FRANGIPANI HOUSE

BERYL GILROY

FRANGIPANI HOUSE

HEINEMANN

Heinemann Educational Publishers
A Division of Heinemann Publishers (Oxford) Ltd
Halley Court, Jordan Hill, Oxford OX2 8EJ

Heinemann: A Division of Reed Publishing (USA) Inc,
361 Hanover Street, Portsmouth, New Hampshire 03801-3912, USA

Heinemann Educational Books (Nigeria) Ltd
PMB 5205, Ibadan
Heinemann Educational Boleswa
PO Box 10103, Village Post Office, Gaborone, Botwsana

FLORENCE   PRAGUE   PARIS   MADRID
ATHENS   MELBOURNE   JOHANNESBURG
AUCKLAND   SINGAPORE   TOKYO
CHICAGO   SAO PAULO

First published by Heinemann Educational Books,
in the Caribbean Writers Series as CWS 37 in 1986
First published in this edition, 1986

British Library Cataloguing in Publication Data

Gilroy, Beryl
Frangipani house.—(Caribbean writers series; 37)
I. Title   II. Series
813 [F]   PR9320.9.G5/

ISBN 0–435–98852–2

Typeset by Activity Ltd, Salisbury, Wilts.
Printed and bound in Great Britain by
Cox & Wyman Ltd, Reading, Berkshire

95 96 97 98   10 9 8 7 6 5 4

In loving memory
Pat Gilroy 1919–1975

I

A strip of road, brown as burnt sugar, and tender as old calico led to a large low house which had become a home for old folk. Aged old folk – black women. All relics of work-filled bygone days. Forty-three of them paying for the privilege of confinement while waiting, waiting, waiting for the 'call from heaven'.

Anyone who came upon the house sitting sleek and comfortable on the town's edge, stopped outside its finely wrought iron gate as if under a spell. It was that kind of house – eloquent, compelling and smug. Sleepy headed windows dressed in frilled bonnets of lace and fine, white cotton, hibiscus shrubs that danced their flower bells to the songs of the wind, and a mammee apple tree that kept the grounds clean by never bearing fruit, marked the house as a place of professional comfort, care and heart's ease.

A circular skirt of closely-cropped grass, with ruched panels of bright low-growing flowers offered familiarity and friendship to passers-by. But it was the ring of frangipani trees, just inside the slender, white painted spears of railings that marked the limits of the grounds, which named the house and caused folk to whisper darkly 'Over yonder – Frangipani House! People dies-out dere! They pays plenty to die-out inside dere! Death comes to lodgers in Frangipani House!'

The women were never objects of derision. Most people were curious about them. Their incarceration was sometimes envied, and often pitied. Some of the women, too demented to care, set out each day on wordless wanderings. Others talked alone as they walked alone, or argued with some long-gone foe or friend, or gestured at those ghosts that somehow learnt to survive the light of day. A few suddenly turned from frenzied laughter to frenzied song. But there were days when a resinous silence seized the house and bound it fast and held it still. It was both a mysterious and an assertive place.

The occupants of Frangipani House were the lucky few – lucky to escape the constipated, self-seeking care which large, poor families invariably provide. After much heart-searching, children who have prospered abroad bought what was considered superior care for their parents, when distance intervened between anguished concern and the day-to-day expression of that concern. Then admission to Frangipani House became an answer to a prayer.

The sole proprietrix and administrator of the home was Olga Trask, a comely, honey-brown predator of a woman, short and crisp, with blue-grey eyes and a full head of coarse black hair. True to history there had been a rampant European among the women of her tribe and it showed in the shape of her nose, and in the eager, seeking hands that would confiscate the copper pennies on the eyes of a corpse. With practised sincerity she professed undying love of her mother who had died in Olga's care. When the old lady had aged to helplessness, Olga returned home, and rather than abandon her mother to cursory care, she bought and developed Frangipani House. She made a convincing job of running the business and when the old woman finally died, Olga's reputation for good works had spread like grass fire. People pointed her out in the street and called her Matron. Not many noticed that she was insatiable for power in a serious and efficient manner. On admission the women placed everything in her care. Those who still felt the pulse of life, however weakly, found soon enough that not only did the walls of the house recede to leave them exposed and vulnerable, but suddenly it compressed them enough to cause consternation before they adjusted to their new surroundings. The hopes and emotions the women shared grew hazy with the passing of time. Finally they disintegrated leaving only faint smudges when they were finally blown away.

Mrs Mabel Alexandrina King, Mama King to all who knew her, had been ailing for a considerable time and her daughters, concerned with the rapid disappearance of their resources as various relatives tried to provide care, telephoned

Miss Trask from New York to obtain a place in Frangipani House for their mother.

'There is no single bed at the moment,' replied Miss Trask. 'Only a single room. Your mother being lady-like would want a room. Old people like doing certain things in private. My own mother, I remember her. She is the same.'

Token, the older of the two girls agreed.

'She will be all right here – good food – good care – morning and evening prayer in case the call comes in the day-time,' assured Miss Trask. The doctor come regular. I pay for that.'

'How much, we have to pay?' Token asked uneasily.

There was a long silence after Miss Trask said, 'Ah well, four – five hundred dollars a month.' 'Five hundred!' 'Yes. you can afford that?' She could hear breathless calculations and even more breathless argument at the end of the telephone, and then just as she was about to ring off, Token cleared her throat and replied 'Ver well. We will pay. But we want white people care for her. We'll come over as soon as we can. We want her house left as it is – in case she want to go back home. My mother is independent and determined. Treat her well – please treat her well.'

Miss Trask pushed the sobs and intercesssions away from her. She was used to them.

'They always coming and they always crying. Damn them! Who they think they are?' she said as she dropped the telephone. She walked quietly and deliberately back to her desk and gave the order to prepare 'the room by the garden.'

'Do anybody know dis Mama King?' she asked her day-duty nurses.

Nurse Douglas, a tall, thin, conscientious village girl who was glad of the work and the status, explained that Mama King had been ill for quite a long time with malaria, then quinsy, then pleurisy.

'I hear the talk. I hear her daughters paying-out all the time. Paying for things the old woman never see nor taste. I feel sorry for all them. It's good she coming here. I hear she did do a lot of good in her young days.'

3

'Hm,' said Miss Trask. 'In that case, see she settle down. Don' go mad. Jus' keep a close eye. Make her feel welcome.'

The very next day Mama King was installed in a tiny room with the minimum of clutter and a fair-sized glass window on one side. The window gave her a close-up of grass and tree and the large iron gate which sometimes locked her in. It also gave a distant view of the world beyond the frangipani trees. Life was pleasantly confined to the house and the well-kept grounds. The strangeness of the routine, the ordered rhythm of life, the cleanliness of everything excited her at first and she slowly regained her health. But after the pleurisy vanished, the urge for freedom reasserted itself as the days passed without variety or change. As a model inmate Mama King was allowed to walk around the grounds reading such notices as 'Keep off the grass,' 'Off limits to residents.' She encountered passages from the psalms or the Book of Proverbs that had been scrawled on the paintwork from time to time, and laughed as she used to laugh with her loved ones not so long ago.

She loved the grass. She remembered its feel underfoot as she walked barefoot to school. Her thoughts swung slowly like the pendulum of a weary clock, and touched those memories of the time she lay beside her husband somewhere out there on the grass. They talked and hoped and planned then, but where was that time now? Buried out there? Gone forever? She touched the grass with the tip of a slippered foot, but Matron's voice swept over her like a fly-whisk.

'You walking on grass Marma King? The sign mean you too, you know!'

The old woman looked up. A strained intensity that became sheer eloquence even as Matron watched, took over her face. 'Don't worry yourself, Marma King. You must feel strange here but you just come ... You get used to it!'

'Why you callin' me Marma King? I am Mama King. Mama mean mother. Don't call me dat stupid name! Marma King! I ask you! What kinda name dat is?'

'You not happy here?' Matron asked. 'You talkin so bad?

4

For a old lady you talkin really bad about everything.'

'Nothin' doin' in here!' The old woman's voice seemed to come from somewhere inside her that had been encrusted with pain.

'I sit down. I rock the chair. I look out. I see the same tree, gasping for breath in the same sun. I see the same cross road where the beggar meet up with them people selling fowl. I see the same scatter of feather and rags like embroidery on the carrion crow bush, where the beggars hang they things. And the time – it nibble away at me life like rat eating cheese. You don't see it going. But you wake up one morning and it all gone. Wha kinda place dis is!'

Mama King suddenly noticed that she was alone – talking to herself. Matron had disappeared. She walked back to her room with discontent biting into her being like a plague of fleas.

Scratching her arm, her leg, her neck, made her conscious of the form of her body. It responded to her in a way that made her aware of being alive in the home, and of the larger awareness of being alive in the world.

Just then Miss Tilley started screaming and as if to ease their own anguish several other old women joined in – their voices blending the guilt, remorse and resentment of old age.

There was nowhere to hide from the screams, they formed an invisible barrier around her. And when at last they stopped she felt compelled to seek out and be grateful for a place of her own. Since her entry into the home, she had begun to see the world through the glass window of her room as was the destiny of many old people. Mr Carey the druggist told her once, 'Too often old people get to see the world through window. To make it interesting – they must pretend it's magic.'

II

Back in her room Mama King could still hear the nurses joking, chatting and discussing the women as they prepared to serve the midday meal. The room was empty save for her own attenuated presence, but the domestic sounds and the voices of youth at work deepened her feelings of isolation. Many women had occupied that room, and yet, and yet they had left nothing. The thought jolted her and brought her face to face with the past and with her present reality.

The film of memory unwound itself revealing moments of pleasure and other things dear to her –

'I was young once – just like them. I go to a fete with Ginchi and we meet two boy. One name Cyril and the round-face one name Danny. They follow us like two dog. I like Danny and the next day I look he out by the market. "I come from New Town Way" he say. "I like you. I think you is nice young girl. I axe 'bout you character. Dey say it good. You want to start friendsing with me?" "He too black" Ginchi Thorley say. "We must wash out we children."'

'"You won't get a better man," me Mama say. But I didn't give a quick yes. I had to know his ways. Maybe he got bad ways who can tell wid a man?'

She smiled as much at her own cleverness as at the bees that buzzed against the glass, but nothing could ease that cutting sense of loss she felt for all the things she had once called her own. Was it not the first time she had sat alone with all her people gone from her? A nurse she had never seen before quietly entered the room and brought her food.

'Mama King,' the nurse said, 'Please eat for me. You not eatin, they say. You want to waste away and turn to jumbie?'

'Not your business what I do,' Mama King replied swiftly. 'What I do is my business.' Glancing at the girl again Mama King noticed something familiar about her. But she could not quite recall it.

'What you name chile?'

'Carol Carey.'

'Carey, the druggist? We use to be good friend with dem! Token was good friends with Julie Carey. Her mother did name Sarah and she was me class-mate in school.'

'My grandma, Mama King. She dead,' said the girl.

'Wish was me.'

'Don't wish dat Mama King. Plenty people want you and care 'bout you.'

'Wha you doin' in dis God forsaken place, chile?'

'I work here sometime – till I ready to go to America – one day. I want to work there. I got plenty pen friends there. Even one of your own family does write me.'

'Hm, I wish they write me! They forget everything bout me. I old now. Just trash to throw out.'

She examined the food carefully as if seeking a hidden object, then sure of its absence, she ate without another word.

'Dis food is like everything else in here. No different. No change. I wish Danny come and take me out of dis place.'

Almost magically she dozed off, and testing the depth at which she slept, some flies danced around the bits of food with which she had decorated her face. She gave herself a sharp tap, jumped awake, walked towards the window and looked out. Nothing had changed but way beyond the trees and close to the grass, she could see and hear footsteps – Danny's footsteps. She recognised them as a musician recognises a calypso, a waltz or a rumba.

'I like Danny first time I see him. But his mother say no he mustn't married yet. Bull must pasture longer than cow. But he like me. He promise me a ring. A nice gold ring!' As she had done many years before she once again wrapped their secret tightly round herself. That way it gave her comfort in bed each night, and sustained her wherever she went each day. And she smiled at it and caressed it at every turn.

'Meet me tonight' Danny say. *'I know you mudder does go to prayer meeting on a Tuesday night. Meet me.'*

'Suppose she turn back.'

7

'She won't turn back. She turn back any time? Why she turn back this time?'

'Suppose she ketch we.'

When all doubt had fallen away, she gave herself to him. Once again she breathed his body, and saw the whites of his eyes, whiter than the clouds high above the cold earth and the triangle of grass on which they lay. Once again she felt the burden of her youth and of her love.

Next day her secret died. She told Ginchi and so lost its warmth next to her breast and in her heart. The memory vanished engulfing something wonderful inside her. She yelled, 'Dis place is a hole. A deep dark hole. They killin' me in here!! I get better long, long time. I want to go home. I can look after meself. Murder!'

'No you can't Marma King,' Matron said with a naked firmness. 'You kind daughters payin' for you. We looking after you now. You old and shaky.'

'Where my dress? I want my dress. I bring plenty dress in here. Where my dress? You thief my dress. My dress is American dress. I will know it. I will drag it off youback.'

'Sit down Marma King,' said Matron is a softer tone than usual. 'Drink this to cool you temper. I'll ask about you Merican Dress. Is dat what you call the material?'

III

Mama King drank what she thought was Coca-Cola and in a few minutes she had dozed off.

'She'll be quiet for a few hours,' Matron assured Nurse Douglas. 'Go and see Miss Mason. She's another one. She read books the same way as she lost her virginity. All those years ago. Energetic and eager. I could just see her.'

Nurse Douglas lowered her eyes. She felt shame going through her like an electric shock. Miss Mason was as old as Matron's mother. What a horrible way to talk of someone so old, so clean and so intelligent.

For a while Nurse Douglas watched while Miss Mason, eighty-nine years old, and lively enough to read and reminisce coherently, eat her meal with studied suspicion, and without spilling.

'I expect one day the Matron would try to poison me,' she said. 'Why, I don't know. Perhaps it's because I'm what she would have liked her mother to have been. I was a school teacher you know.'

'Yes,' said Nurse Carey who stood beside her. 'I heard how wonderful you were in the school and in the town – helping all the poor people.'

Nurse Douglas came closer. 'Miss Mason were you ever in love?' she asked. 'In love enough to have a child?'

Miss Mason motioned Miss Douglas even closer. 'Time for truth has come,' she said. 'As a matter of fact. No. I never did anything with men, boys or girls if such a thing is possible. Nobody was good enough for me. "No," said my mother, "men are evil. Men are bad. Men are the devil." I never married. I was never in love except in my imagination. I could build a man like you build a house and then fall in love. It is true that one of my pupils adopted me and pays for my keep. Besides,' she winked, 'You and the doctor could check me out

9

when I kick the bucket.'

She laughed so prettily that Nurse Douglas, unable to stop herself, laughed with her.

'I have a nice man – separate from his wife,' confided the nurse. 'It's the best I can get. I will have a child later on, when the divorce come through.'

'Do the best you can – when you can,' said the old lady. She got off her bed and on her strong calfless legs made her way to the trolley to change her book.

'I want another romance,' she said. 'A true romance then tonight I can dream of things you people indulge in. If I were young again I would love every man who was willing until he screamed for mercy.'

There was a sudden scurrying in the space outside Mama King's door. The nurses could hear her talking to herself, or muttering and some times crying out as if in agony. Nurse Douglas and Nurse Tibbs banged on the door in turn.

'Don't,' pleaded Nurse Carey. 'She's only talking. All old people talk like that. She's saying the things she never said. That is old age!'

'I wonder if reading a romance to her would help,' chirruped Miss Mason. 'That's what happens when women can't have something they once had. That's my imagination at work again.'

'Go to your bed, Miss Mason,' Nurse Tibbs said sharply. 'Go and read your book. Later I will put some jam on your mouth and you can pretend Prince Charming is waking you up with a kiss.'

'That will be nice, Nurse Tibbs,' Miss Mason replied, 'I shall be much obliged to you. Please will you give this to the terrier dog? It's a bit of chewing gum. I can't eat it. It extracts my false teeth. We have to have mercy on that poor dog. It's Matron's.'

Mama King was talking in her room like a drunken preacher. Nurse Douglas, her ear to the door, heard her voice distinctly. The walls of the room precluded everything but the act in which the old lady was involved.

10

'I go to look for Danny to say I with chile. Then I lost meself. Branches trying to grabble me and the sky over me with stars like silver money. Danny! I holler Danny! Then he fine me and lay me back against a tree – and wet me face and lovey-dovey with me and put me to rest.'

'Few days pass then he come talk to me mother. We live together and when Token born we married. Token was fair-skin like Danny mother. Now I don't know where Danny gone. I never hear bout him but I remember his footsteps dancing like drumsticks at the wedding.'

Matron came scurrying. 'Out of the way everybody,' she said. 'That old lady is a trial but at least she is clean. I don't have to change her sixty times a day.' Keys clanking, she opened the door. On seeing Matron Mama King walked towards the window and menacingly continued her soliloquy.

'My brother is a strong iron-build man; he kill man or woman who take advantage of his generation. Danny might kill too. Ginchi say he in Aruba looking for work, but my brother live in America. He name Abel. He send for me children but I never want to go there. He like Token when he see she photo. But Token was a spiteful baby. She never want to wean. Token cry whole day and whole night. Then she stop and drink the pap.'

'I use to do plenty work – bake, wash, sell, scrub, domestic work. Me and Danny never row. He keeping all the money. Then one day he disappear. When he disappear I find Cyclette in me belly.'

'Come on Mama King,' said Matron. 'Don't look back, Danny gone! Gone like the Calypso say "to Cove and John". It could mean any place, any country.'

'Danny ain't gone! Danny here.' She placed her hand over her heart. 'You know,' she said, 'A bird can sing but it can't cry. A bird can feel sad like I feel, I wish I was a bird! When I wear black dress and go to funeral, I mourning for my feelings, and happy days that gone forever. I never see Danny again. He so handsome. He never hear 'bout Cyclette. Danny just disappear.'

'Well Marma King. We all have cross to bear. You got. Me got. Everybody got cross to bear. It no use complaining to me. Get to know God. Cry on God shoulder.' The resentment in her voice could have roasted a dozen yams, but Mama King was conscious only of the searing loss of fellowship she felt at

11

that moment, and moaned, 'I want Danny. Danny gone and I don' know. Where Danny gone?'

Then like a bird calling for its mate she called and called for Danny. She kept at it long after she was sure no reply would reach her.

IV

Miss Mason stealthily dressed herself in all her nighties, her head scarves and her hats. The nighties gave her frail body a comically layered look and the hats were incongruously piled one on top of the other, making her already shrunken features more wizened than ever. Then as if someone had quietly actuated an old gramophone and an ancient record, she started to sing and dance in a stilted, rudimentary manner.

'I like a nice cup of tea in the morning. I like a nice cup of tea with my tea.' The nurses' laughter rang around the room. Miss Mason was encouraged by it and lifting up all her nighties to show a dark-brown flabby bottom, she turned to the four points of the compass and wiggled in brief, timid bursts.

'That's what I did when my mother was not looking,' she yelled. 'Like a ball of twine, I rolled my botty round, and round. Hip! Hip! Hooray! There's a black girl in the ring. Tra la – Tra la la.'

'That's enough, Miss Mason,' said Nurse Tubbs. 'We not your mother. So lie down and you can sing and wiggle in bed. You want a heart attack?'

The old woman climbed into bed, still wearing all her nightclothes, scarves and hats. The nurses waited patiently for the time when sleep overwhelmed her before they would undress her.

'We must make sure she don't do that again,' said Nurse Douglas. 'She fake-happy that one. Paper happy! When we undress her, we have to hide them things so she don't find them.'

'But her antics make the day go quick, you know. I like her,' replied Nurse Tibbs appreciatively. 'I really like her. The other day she offer to teach me to play bridge. But we play Thirty-One – three cents a game and she beat me too! All the while we playing, Miss Tilley keep on muttering "Gamblin is an abomination unto the Lord". Miss Mason does make me laugh. She say "The Lord is everybody, God – father. He like a little Abomination in his rum".'

'Nurse Tibbs!' shouted Mama King, 'I wan' go outside. The day look clean. All its sins wash away. And look at dem trees. They look so nice!'

The frangipani trees were laden with sweet-scented orange-coloured flowers, but the most wanton of their petals took short rides astride the wind and slowly swirled to the ground. They had the appearance of snippets of ribbon strewn across a green baize carpet by wilful hands.

The more keenly Mama King watched the petals dancing and gliding on the wind the more memories escaped from her, causing her mind to scurry and scamper after them. Were those memories about her girls or about Miss Tilley's house that smelt of rotting oranges? She shook her head as if trying to jerk memory from some secluded corner of her brain – out of the crevice in which time had buried it but the memory stayed in its grave. Nurse Tibbs watched her and wondered what was going on. She continued her circular walk around an area heaped with petals, and picked some up and then, like a child caught doing some forbidden thing, she shyly dropped them again. She walked towards the low shed and scraped off those petals that adorned its bald, corrugated pate. Once more she thought of Danny. The house in which they first lived had such a roof, and when the sun heated it to boiling point, large, black spiders came out, seeking shade. But she walked with Danny when work was done and sat on the clean sand, and listened to the river chortling as it flowed, and watched the mangrove trees motionless in the dull, leaden darkness.

She hardly noticed when the memory she had been seeking came out of hiding. But she greeted it with a welcome smile. Of course, the colour reminded her of her daughters, both dressed in orange coloured costumes for the school play. She stared out into the distance, allowing spools of recollections to unwind.

'They did want Token for Snow White. But she too tall. She make a good dwarf, though. She say everything she had to say. Everybody clap. I feel so proud. I take in plenty washing to rig them out for the play and when it happen I forget the rheumatism in me hand from the hot an' cold water. The teacher so please wid Token. I notice how she grown – fullin' out and then all of a sudden, Token sick. She wouldn't eat a thing – only drink, an even that. She get fine – fine – fine! I say "God if you wan' she, take she", and I watch she turnin' to skeleton before me eyes. Then somebody tell me 'bout Maraj – a old, coolie man who know 'bout sickness.

'Where he live no bus does go. So Token an' me, we go by Donkey Cart for five hours and we reach there. He look at Token – she got nara. She guts twist. It easy for children guts to twist. He 'noint Token belly – she holler for mercy, but he 'noint her two more time. She eat dat same night. I kneel down in front of Maraj. I say "I ain' got money – only dis brooch. It solid gold. Take it."'

'"Keep your brooch. We all is poor people," he tell me. "Feed ten beggar one for every year you chile livin.' I don' wan' money. Tonight I go to sleep. Tomorrow I can wake up somewhere else. Thank God for everything."'

'People always good to me. The teacher never charge me a cent. She teach Token for nothing. Then she teach Cyclette. When I ask her about money – how much I got to pay she say, "Who talkin' 'bout payin! They will remember me when I get old. Cast your bread on the water. Dat's what the Bible say". It look like yesterday when Token pass for nurse and Cyclette for secretary. Because they had a little complexion, they get work easy. Token was a good nurse. The patient dem like her and Cyclette could make a typewriter sing, laugh – run and jump. Only yesterday they was little. Danny would proud of them. Poor Danny – I wonder where he stay now. Dead and gone. I believe so. Nobody see him or meet him. Even people who been to Aruba. I wonder where Danny gone?'

'Mama King,' Matron shouted from the door. 'You staring like you mad! People who stare like that have empty, idle mind. Why don't you think positive, instead of standing around and staring at nothing.'

'Since I come here I look, but all I see is what past and gone.

15

You have now. All I have is long ago. Go and count you money. It got old people blood on it!'

In a mocking, over-deferential manner she curtsied to the Matron, then twisting her body through the small space that the Matron's bulk had left unoccupied, she went back into her room to rock her feelings to rest. She walked round and round the bed and then once again, unable to resist its beckoning, lay down and closed her eyes.

'Matron think I doing nothing,' she said quietly to herself 'but thinking is hard work.'

'I sit down and my whole life pass before me – like a film at a picture show. I get so tired but yet I can't stop. And everybody think my mind empty, my head empty and my heart empty. I see people, dead and gone, walking and talking and young. And out of my old worn out body, a young woman walk out and life is like roll of new cloth waiting to roll out.'

She fell asleep.

She woke around dusk but she did not get up, and when Nurse Douglas entered her room she faked sleep.

'Come on, Mama King. I know you wake up. You want cocoa-tea or coffee?'

'I want cocoa-tea.'

While she sipped the cocoa, a flight of blue Sakis hurrying home in the dying light caught her eyes. The sun, plump and comfortable behind wisps of gossamer-mauve clouds, sank slowly out of sight. It was the end of another day.

'I wonder how long I been here. How long they keeping me here! How long I going to live Lord? I wonder how long?'

'Nurse,' she called, 'I want to go home. I miss everything.'

'Mama King, you lucky. Life is a treadmill. You been on it for years and years. You daughters push you off. Don't grumble. Don't complain. Count your blessings.'

Mama King sucked her teeth. 'You don' teach you grandmother to suck egg. I wan' go home, I wan' pen and paper to write me daughters. They must come and take me out of this terble place.'

'Well, tell you what, when you mind clear you can write.

16

Wait till tomorrow. I will get you pen and paper and I will post the letter for you.'

'I wan' the paper now,' Mama King insisted. 'And the pen, and the ink.' Lucid, aggressive and determined, she kept on demanding writing materials until the nurse complied. She wrote a message to Token like a child given lines for punishment.

'Token, I want go home. I better. I hate this place.

Token, I want go home. I better. I hate this place.'

She wrote until all the lines on the paper were covered. She had written it thirty times. Then she addressed the envelope and sealed in the letter allowing the nurse to take it from her and put it in her pocket.

'I will post it for you,' Nurse Douglas promised. 'I going home just now.'

Mama King had doubts about the letters she asked the nurses to post. She never received any replies and every complaint she made was either swept aside like rotten wood in a rough wind, or ignored as if she complained in a foreign language. The women were expected to think themselves privileged and lucky to be under Matron's care.

The timid knock on her door went unanswered until she gathered her limbs, her wits, her feelings about her as if she was picking up shells out of loose sand.

Miss Mason stood there wearing a slipper on one foot, and a shoe on the other and on her head a battered cloche hat that could have come out of a hobo's pocket.

'Hello,' Miss Mason twittered. 'How are you today. I came to see you.'

'You sure? I see you got a bag. You come to thief again? You thief me orange, me guava, me biscuit and whatever else you could lay your hands on.'

Miss Mason frowned. 'I only took your banana. I'm keeping everything just in case Matron drops dead and there's no food for us. Then you'll all have to come and beg food of me.'

'I see,' Mama King replied tentatively.

'I came to tell you about your husband. You always worry about him. Well he's all right. He's across water and there is gold too. Don't get married again and you'll be ship-shape to get to the end of time. He loves you just as much as ever.'

'Don' talk about love. Is something you think about when you young and then you live it through your children when you old,' snapped Mama King.

'Just as you wish. I thought I'll give you the message.' Miss Mason's eyes revolved around the room. There was nothing edible for her to pilfer but the clatter of dishes drew her to the dining room.

Mama King resumed her seat by the window, and on the grass outside, a patchwork of events from her life lay sprawled before her in a kind of half-light.

'Since Danny gone my feelings for men shrivel like grass in dry weather. Ben Le Cage did come roun' once or twice but he is like mucka-mucka*. He make you scratch yourself morning, noon and night with worry. He live wid woman after woman – get chile after chile and as fas' as he get them, he forget 'bout them. I can' believe he get them normal. He mus' get fed up doin' the same thing so much time with so much women. He never think 'bout God dat man! I didn't take notice of him. I say I is a married woman – I aint one of you hole an' corner. He didn't like that. "You got two girl children", he say. "Who will take you wid two girl? Boy more useful. Girl is trouble. Before they twenty they go and get belly." I chase him out when he say that. He want to bring bad luck on my two girl.'

The cadences of her own voice seemed to lull her into a deep sleep. Only the muffled sounds of moans and sighs that seemed to be fragments of anguish rising from the graveyard inside her, synchronised with her breathing. 'She never dreamt', she said. She had never been able to recall a single dream but that evening one stuck in her mind and frightened her.

She was a child again walking demurely beside her mother along a road stretching far into the distance. There was no one else in sight but she could hear voices singing familiar tunes. The road suddenly became liquid and there she was

*A plant, the juice causes itching when in contact with skin.

swimming in the cool, chattering water. But her mother had disappeared and there was Matron scowling and scolding and shouting at her. Everything happened in an instant. She had grown old and Danny, as young as when she last saw him, had appeared on the scene. She rushed up to him but he eyed her with suspicion and cutting resentment.

'I don' want you,' he said. 'You old! You ugly! I want this nice clean skin woman.'

He embraced Matron and then pushed his wife out of their way. She felt a searing pain on her shoulder where he had touched her and she screamed. The nurses rushed in. Her face, covered with sweat emphasised the astonishment and pain in her eyes. 'I dream,' she whispered, 'I dream ....'

'It's only a nightmare, Mama King,' comforted Nurse Carey. 'It's gone now. Only me and you here now.'

Mama King still sobbed. Her heart was so full of hatred, although she did not know for whom, that at the slightest touch she would split open like a ripe calabash dropped on stone.

'Ginchi,' she called, 'Ginchi!' But her friend had long since gone home. She rushed to the window. There was nothing to see – just a slither of moon and whipped egg-white clouds scurrying away to the other side of the globe.

More than anything else she wanted work. She always had a special relationship with work. Her body needed it as it needed food and clothes. And now, time and life, her daughters and the matron had all conspired to deprive her of her faithful friends, work and hardship. She felt as though they had punched and kicked her and given her many terrible blows.

She began once more to prowl round and round the room like a caged animal. Even the window had clouded over. She ran her fingers along the sill and so found comfort and peace. Why had work deserted her for no reason to speak of? True, she had been sick, and even getting older but since when work turn its back on poor, old people?

'If work come now and stan' up before me, I give her a big-big cuffing. Lord, how wonderful are they works! All works belong to God.'

19

V

The next Sunday was visiting day, when Miss Ginchi, Mama King's girlhood friend, paid her weekly visit. Mama King identified Sunday as the day when her hair was combed, her false teeth soaked in cleansing solution, and when Nurse Douglas paid more than scant attention to her personal hygiene.

At precisely three o'clock, a quiet dignity descended like a dust-cloud, and enveloped the place. Some inmates eyed the door in quick furtive glances, but for others waiting for visitors was like waiting for the eighth day of the week. Too fractious inmates were suitably calmed down, and lay like carved ebony figures in a state of suspended animation. Miss Mason, cuddling her doll, sucked voraciously at her comforter but her love for dressing up was encapsulated in the pair of red ribbon bows on her almost hairless head.

Mama King wore a floral blue and white dress and flat-heeled white shoes. She looked relaxed and the years seemed to fall away from her. Some children in the distance caught her eye. Was it Solomon and Cindy come back to her? A sudden stabbing pain in her heart symbolised all the longing she felt for the presence of all her grandchildren. Thoughts of having them young again and dependent on her, ruptured something inside her. It was rage. Rage that had been so deeply buried, it had undergone a total change, to become concern, commiment, solicitude and even love. For some reason tears were close.

'They never ask me if I want to be mother and father again and again. Nobody ever ask me! They just make it so I got to do it. Token make her bed, but she want me to lie down with her. Seventeen years old, and one month in America. She got a good work and everything but no, she got married to a man no better than addle egg. "He nice, Mama. He nice. I did know him from back home. I gettin' a baby." That's all she writing to tell me. So she married. Soon the man turn. He was a scamp. Only

20

wan' money to gamble. He …' She stopped as if her thinking had been switched off.

Her friend had entered the room. She too wore smart Sunday clothes. No one could have guessed that she was well into her seventieth year and able to help and work and care for much younger others. She was like a thin piece of black string with a face on which her various schemes had left their mark. Her arms and legs seemed to go on for ever. A small black hat with a cluster of iridescent feathers on the side, rested on top of her grey hair, parted in three neat clumps. And her dress with its flowing gored skirt was just right for a visit to Frangipani House.

'Mabel,' she said. 'I come to see you. You all right? I think about you all the time. Wondering what these black-white doing you.'

Mama King gave a fleeting smile. Like water poured on sand. It never came to anything before it disappeared. Then suddenly as if she was being tickled by unseen hands, she burst into a loud laugh.

'What you laughing?' asked Miss Ginchi. 'What you laughing? Laugh today, cry next day! You laughing because I dress up! Dress up like a jubilee craupaud.'

'I remember the time when Tilley come out-a trench in she thin voile dress. It wet and it stick on she like crazy embroidery. The overseer eye pop out when he see she. At dead of night she go to see him. The next minute the belly show.'

Ginchi joined in the laughter.

'You know how Tilley stay,' she said quizzically. 'She say, when she see goodlooking man, "I mus' make a child if I got chance." Only when she making a baby, she happy. When she got chile inside her, she feel hopeful – she look to the future. Children is future. Children make you look forward. When she makin' a chile, everything working inside she, mind heart and soul. She happy. Six boy she make – all growed and gone. They look after she. No man to mix up things. Man does really mix up things. They do one thing. You do something else! Man and woman together is woe in the worl'!' When Tilley see empty shoes it mus' have foot.'

21

'Ginchi. I never hear from Token or Cyclette. Not a word! I write but I don't get answer. Somebody taking me letter.' Mama King looked fearfully around.

'Don't frighten,' consoled her friend. 'You 'member Carlton. He is laundry-boy here. I tell him to keep his ears open for talk about letter. Don't frighten. I goin' to say something when time come right.'

Mama King listened with her face and her eyes but her mind was treading its own path.

'What happen to Token husband? I forget how they call him. He disappear when the second belly show. She stranded in a foreign country but Abel come to rescue her and send her home to me. Abel was a man. He never forget family. He buy me house for me. He give me money till he dead. Then he leave the money for Solo to study doctor. Is then I turn burden to the girls. They children never burden on me.'

Miss Ginchi coughed. She was always sorry for Mabel when she went back inside herself. How many times had she felt the same searing sorrow of heart from Mabel who could sit and stare for hours, then cry a little, smile a little, and then give a little weary groan?

'You know Ginchi,' she said, after a long silence. 'I don' want old age. I don' want to burden nobody. But who can choose? Clear as day I can remember when Token came home wid Solo. She had Cindy in her belly and she stay till Cindy born. Solo cry a lot but he soon get to know everybody. When Token go back to her work in America, he didn't cry for her. He cry for me. He grow so quick. He like to go to school. He read all the book he mother send. The teacher say he got good head for learnin'. Then Token divorce the father. Cindy favour the father. No matter how you beat her, no matter how you talk, she go her own way. I sen' her back to her mother when she twelve year, but I keep Solo till he pass his exam. I wonder where Solo is. You know Ginchi, all my family disappear from me!'

'Children grows and then they goes looking for nest to feather. You can' keep them,' Miss Ginchi said sadly. 'And we gets old.'

There were voices outside the window and a young couple walked hand in hand in the distance.

'She used to walk with Danny and then run fast across the field. He could never catch her. Life was good in those days. Laughing was easy. Tilley came in the yard with her six and in next to no time, they would build a fire and roast yam and potatoes and corn. Then Ben would banjo and the children would dance for pennies.'

'I want go home Ginchi,' she said weakly, 'I write to Token plenty time and axe the nurse to post it. I never get answer.'

'Carlton, my grandson, does work in the laundry,' said Miss Ginchi. 'I tell you already.'

The nurse came in with a tray of food.

'You want something to eat, Mama King,' asked Nurse Tibbs pleasantly.

As she busied herself, Miss Ginchi could see the folded bit of paper peeking out of her pocket. Recognising Mama King's writing she gently pulled it out.

'I goin' Nurse – look after Mama King for me. She all the friend I got. You apron is a little dirty. You wear it for two day. A nurse shouldn' do dat.'

When she opened the door, the little terrier that had been frisking outside it rushed into the room. Mama King did not encourage the Matron's dog. She ordered it out of her room, but it soon sneaked back sniffing and scouting for crumbs. Many of the women despised the dog for living in the home. All those they had known lived outside and slept in an out-house or a corner of the kitchen when it rained. Disgusted they watched Matron making a child of it, talking to it and feeding it good meat. Yet it never missed a chance to behave like one of its species, lifting its leg at every tree and scavenging for food. It barked incessantly on visiting days and only settled down when the last visitor had departed.

Mama King sympathised with the dog. 'It can't help itself,' she told Tilley. 'None of us in here can help ourself. Poor Dog. You wouldn' like it if Matron own you. You will act stupid jes like the dog. It got to bark. It got to act mad.'

VI

With the disappearance of the last visitors the pulse of life returned to Frangipani House. Both staff and inmates felt release and showed it by discussing the afternoon's happenings, or watching as the night dropped in an opaque, star-crested blanket over the land. The sounds of the darkness were complementary too – crickets ruthlessly chirping, frogs croaking a cacophony and fresh young laughter from young people whose hopes had not yet become experience. The dog ran into its basket and, exhausted, fell asleep.

Mama King thought of all the distance she had walked in the life, all the loads of wood and bags of charcoal, buckets of water, trays of washing and heavy fruit she had carried on her single, strong head, which in spite of everything had kept its shape. Feeling her head as if to reassure herself that it had not been changed in any way by over-use and years of faithful service, she marvelled at its strength.

Through the window she glimpsed golden sparks where courting candleflies stopped to wait, and moths, determined to approach the tiny bulb of light in her room, beat against her window and then fell like leaves to earth. At last as the muscles of her legs gave up, she stopped walking and carefully placed her head under the pillow, her mind twittering like a bird, while sleep refused all her attemps to woo it. Memories emerged from all those cracks of heart where they lurked in confusion. With the pillow over her head, she tried to trap a portion of the darkness as she did when a child. Then the darkness lost its power and lay quietly beside her.

The fussing sounds of a baby came at her as if from the centre of her being. *'Cindy,' she whispered, choking with pleasure. 'Cindy, you come back!'* But the mysterious baby had vanished and she was still alone. Only the nurses in brief respite played cards outside.

'You own children bring their children and put them in your lap, in your hand, and in your heart as well. You struggle with them, care them, bathe them, cook for them, look after them when they sick. Be mother, father and gran to them. They one day, sudden, sudden, they come, grabble them up and take them miles away over the ocean waters. They leave a hole in you life and in you heart God himself can't patch up.'

'Token come hurry, hurry. She pack up Cindy and Solo take them in a hurry. She write few line to say Cindy gone to school. Then Cindy write. She write, "Momma married again," she say. "Solo don't live here. He live wid Uncle Abel; Momma got another baby but it died. We happy. You should see the food they throw away in this country. Is a sin and a shame." Them two children I build my life around. Token take them without so much as a by your leave. No, I send them back because Cindy too own way. Cindy too own way.'

Nurse Carey, the night nurse said, 'Mamma King, try and get some sleep. You will be tired tomorrow. Try and sleep. It nearly twelve o'clock. Midnight! Jumbie Hour!'

'You can't force sleep. It come when it like. I trying but when me mind take off, it travel to all corners of me life like a rowing boat on tumbling water ...'

'Is who drownded? One of Cyclette boy drownded in the pond when I go to wash clothes with them. Which one? Oh yes it was Boyson – short and square-build. He was five or six. He was little strange in the head. Never stop to reason. Never stop to work things out. He body turn big but the mind in it stay small. I at the pond with them. The other two picking mango. What Boyson doin' in the pond I never know. The next thing I know – I jump in feeling in the water and shoutin' till I find him. I put him on the grass. He dead, dead, dead! Marcey run and call Ginchi and them other people. Gussie pump the ches' – pump the ches' – to make him breathe – but only water come out of he ears, he nose, he mouth. Weed all over he head and face.

'I think 'bout Cyclette. What she tell me? "Mama you neglect me children. Mama you prefer Token children?" Sick with worry. Then Cyclette come for the burying. She see me condition. "Mama," she say. "Don't blame yourself. That boy never right in the head. My husband did not wan' him. He give me pills to drink. Is not your fault. Is me husband and the pills fault, Boyson so stupidity – can't tell wood from

25

water." *She hold on to me and we bawl together. After that I get over the death but I still think of Boyson – I use to beat him when he eat worm, and fly and dead marabunta. I never think he mad. I think he bad. Poor Boyson – dead and gone to he maker.'*

The memory exhausted her. She dozed and then rapid loud snores leapt out from under the sheet. She was sleeping now.

'Some of these old people have a hard time with their conscience,' said Miss Agnes to Nurse Carey as they sat drinking midnight cocoa together. Nurse Carey sipped her cocoa, thinking of Miss Tilley in Room Two. She had six children by five men. Gossip said she had been a beauty – dark, smooth-skinned and statuesque. Men fell at her feet. But they never loved her for long. They found her, so it was said, insatiable and so they fled, leaving her with the children they gave her.

'Whatever she did to them, her children cared 'bout her. Look at the way they pay for her! Send her everything she want.' Nurse Carey said incredulously, 'They pay whatever they have to pay.'

'I think Mama King funny – so sulky. She must give a man a hard time. I ain't sure how I feel about her,' Nurse Agnes said screwing up her face as if she tasted something bitter.

'I don't know, my family know all of them. Her daughter is my Godmother. When Mama King husband left her, she worked – turned her hand to anything. Don't judge, you don't know. You always think bad 'bout people.'

Nurse Agnes pulled another face.

The old woman was now deeply asleep but Agnes, anxious to go home, began her chores early. The doctor was due to visit. Good impressions were imperative.

'Mama King, wake up!' she said. The old woman did not respond. In a show of power, Agnes pulled at the pillow. At that moment Nurse Douglas entered. She gasped at the sight of Agnes' unkindness.

'What the hell you doing?' she snapped. 'Leave her in peace. Let her sleep. You go help in the kitchen before I tell Matron what you do! You ain't trained, so try and learn.'

Agnes sucked her teeth and disappeared into the kitchen.

Mama King lay in a pleasant half-awake state, with her mind still running backwards over time.

She was a girl again – fishing with Aunty Lula on a sun-and-shadow day at Elmer creek. They were under some tall trees. Flies were plentiful and the fish jumped to catch those that had the effrontery to skim the surface of the water in their search for insects.

'Throw your line,' Aunty Lula said. 'Fish jumping! You will catch! Jumping fish is hungry fish!' She sat expectant. After a while there was a gentle nibbling on the end then a tug. The fish had taken the hook. She pulled it out – a little oval fish – tail on one end, little hungry mouth on the other. The scales glinted in the sunshine. Her aunt showed her how to free the fish. There was blood on both their hands.

'Yes,' said her aunty 'even fish got blood. Everything got blood.' When she fried her congo fish and ate it, she thought of its blood until she saw the delicate beauty of its bones.

She sat up in bed. The clock struck eight 'morning-time'. Time for her shower and her breakfast. People were speaking in hushed voices. Miss Tilley had died during the night.

'She went to bed OK, tell everybody good night OK, do everything OK,' said Nurse Douglas. 'Then she die. Nobody hear a sound. Ah well. Thy will be done. She had a good time in this world.'

Mother Turvey began to sob. 'Is me nex. I know is me nex. Oh God I so frighten'. Dead does come softily, softily like a thief. I frighten' to dead. O God help me.'

'You got your religion Miss Turvey,' said Nurse Douglas. 'Think about Heaven. It nice – full of milk and honey.'

'This is the first good place I ever get. This is the first time I feel peaceful inside. Oh God spare me! Spare me! Give me this heaven till I reach four hundred.' She sobbed uncontrollably.

Mama King hugged her. 'Don't talk no more, Olga Turvey. Trust God. He take you when he want you. He is the heavenly husbandman. Sure you will see his holy face.'

Miss Turvey nodded and dried her tears. 'I got plenty

blessing but I still worry. There is plenty people begging and starving. Why I worryin'? I don't know. Why?' She smiled broadly and just as a child would kiss another, Mama King kissed her and then went off to shower.

The coldness of the water did not inhibit her desire to talk to herself.

'Olga Turvey right to frighten dead. She got to suffer what she do. Her grandson – the school teacher one, give the young girl chile. She deny the chile. She put her hand in the fire and swear the boy innocent. The girl suffer nine long month till the baby born. Turvey dress up in her Sunday-go-to-meeting to go and inspect the baby. She look from head to face. Nothing – belly and back. Nothing – hand, nothing – foot, nothing but the toe – the big toe in particular – the spitting image of her grandson big toe. Now she crying because dead coming. She got to suffer. I wonder where dat chile gone now? Olga Turvey spoil a young, young boy. But now is no time to think 'bout that.'

She dried the front of her body but finding the back difficult she sung out for the nurse who promptly responded.

'Don't rub me so hard. Me skin ain't make out a concrete. It ain't hard like courida wood either. Is skin, same as you skin – even if it look like dry-up boulanger.'

'Please Mama, don't be difficult. I'm being gentle with you.'

'Yes with you hand rough like corn husk. You used to skin alligator wid it?'

'Mama, your trouble is you forget how to appreciate. How to say thanks. I feel pleased if you say a little thank-you now and then.'

Mama King seemed to have frozen in time and was now by the sea. The wind blew across her face. It was January.

'The wind so cold, Dan,' she said. *'It trade wind, blowing from different place. Some place goes cold with snow and ice. Winter I believe they calls it.'*

'I love sea water. You can't see where it come from and where it go. It like life and death. It keep going on. High tide is like when things good. Neap tide, like when they bad. Sometime the water so smooth – the moon make it look like gold.'

They walked across the sand, across the shadows and through the softly shimmering light. They stopped to rest and then the moment was gone.

'Wipe me back,' she said curtly. 'You call yourself a nurse and you can't wipe people back?' She thought of Tilley alive last week and dead this week. Moaning last night, dead tonight. She imagined her in her shroud pinned down, trapped in those clothes like the flies they used to pin with thorns to the walls of the mud hut near the field where they walked as girls. How pretty life was then! She felt trapped – like a bee in a bottle.

VII

Wednesday – the day of Miss Tilley's funeral: she was to be taken from the house to her family home. There was no chapel in Frangipani House but a room, called the 'dead-room' was tastefully decorated with flowers and artefacts of white protestantism.

The women entered diffidently in ones and twos, to pay their respects. Mama King walked in alone. She wanted to be alone, with her friend lying there present, yet absent, without motion and without action. She recited a blessing her old teacher had taught her for her grandmother's burial.

'I leave you in the care of God. He will protect you on your way to heaven. May your soul never wander and may you find eternal peace.' Then in a voice still tuneful, still able to express what she felt, she sang Tilley's favourite hymn:

'Abide with me, fast falls the eventide
The darkness deepens, Lord with me abide.'

'Stop!' shouted Miss Mason from the door. 'It's too thin. Let me call the others to join in. Miss Turvey is here already. I'll call the others. Let us blend our voices in a thick, heavenly sound.'

'I 'ent comin' in,' said Miss Turvey. 'I can't smell dead-wash people. I sayin' goo'bye from here. Goo'bye Tilley. Goo'bye. Thick or thin I 'ent coming in.'

Mama King placed her hand on Tilley's brow and said tremulously:

'When other helpers fail and comforts flee
Help of the helpless, oh, abide with me.'

She felt certain of her own mortality, like Tilley, wearing an elaborate white nylon shroud with her favourite flowers sprinkled over. She was at peace, forever – her soul a rainbow spanning heaven, and earth.

Her relatives had by now arrived and as they escorted the

coffin out of Frangipani House, Matron asked one of them curtly:

'Who goin' to send the telegram to her children in London – you or me?'

'Tilley gone for good,' Mama King mused. 'She live secretive. She dead secretive. She never tell anybody anything important. You know she dead when you see her going to her burying. I wish today was my day.'

'Don't say that, Mama King. Life is sweet,' said Matron.

'Not mine. It's not worth a single cent.'

The sky was overcast, promising rain. The gardener, a morose man, stopped to watch the cortège, crossed himself, and then, helped by Carlton the laundry boy, tended the young yam plants, while Matron's dog chased butterflies that, feeling the dampness in the air hurried to shelter under the leaves. The clouds opened up – suddenly, eagerly forming rivulets that would conquer and overcome where they could.

From her window Mama King watched their intricate criss-crossings and their power over the debris that was compelled to follow where they led. The bits of straw, wood shavings rushing about like delinquents on the run, broken match sticks, none of these engaged her attention. Only a picture card at the mercy of the rushing water held her gaze. 'That card like me. Going wherever rough water push it.' Now picture side up, the card had no control over its route or its fate. It came to rest behind a stone but the respite was brief. There it was again – water-logged and disintegrating, raindrops falling upon it like stones and seeking truly to destroy it.

Mama King cupped her head in both hands and closed her eyes. When she opened them again, the window was clear. Everything had vanished. 'Lord help me,' she prayed, biting her lips to conceal the quivering. 'A devil addling up my head. The sun so bad, it killin' and shrivellin'. The rain so bad it floodin' and drowndin'. Lord help me.'

She stood rigid. Her fingertips pressed into the window-sill. And there she stayed, her mind a cauldron of emotions until

Nurse Douglas sang out:

'Mama King. A visitor to see you. He talking to Matron just to make sure. Then he want to see you.'

Mama King was thrown in a state of speculative anxiety. As different people flashed through her mind she shook her head and murmured 'm-m-no m-m.'

'Don't look so distracted,' the nurse said. 'Put on something nice. You must look presentable when an old sweet-man come back.'

'M-m,' said Mama King. 'I only did have the one.'

As she spoke the terror of uncertainty seized her. What if Danny came back? Would she want him? Who could this person be? Who would come out of the forest of years that was her past to visit her?

Entering the room as if the floor had suddenly become sticky underfoot she tried hard to control her curiosity. The head alone laid the reappearance of Danny to rest. He had loose, jet black hair. This man wore a thin cap of grey-white peppercorns, his skull showing in the many bald patches.

Her eyes ranged over him, loitering wherever recognition lurked, but still his identity eluded her. Miss Mason, as spectacularly dressed as usual, entered the room sipping sorrel drink from a glass that was revoltingly stained and cloudy. Her clothes higgledy-piggledy about her made her look like a scarecrow that had abandoned its vigil in a cornfield.

'Hello,' she chirped. 'I didn't see a man come in. Here you are. Drink my sorrel drink.'

'No, oh no,' he replied. 'I won't deprive you of what is yours.'

A distant memory stirred. The voice was familiar. Mama King turned her head slowly as if listening with each ear in turn.

'Don't you remember me, Mabel? Ben Le Cage. I've come home, to see you all perhaps for the last time. We are getting on in years, you know!'

'But he live in America,' Mama King said. 'He been there

32

many generation gone!'

'Oh, Mabel. Here I am and glad to see you!'

'What I want to know is what you want! Ben Le Cage only want one thing.'

'Mabel. We are old people now. All the fire gone out. Years pass. You get tired. You settle down. Then old age take over.'

'If you be Ben Le Cage. Tell me what happen tother day at Elmer Crick!'

Ben Le Cage scratched his head with a knobbly, bejewelled finger. 'If I remember rightly,' he said. 'We were a party of youg people indulging in a great deal of folly since youth and folly go together. Like bread and butter. We were skylarking, taking liberties with one another.'

'You didn't think dat when Tilley lay you down in ant's nest. When the ants take over you backside you cuff she face and burst-up she lip, and cover she clothes with blood. Her good clothes, too…!' If Ben Le Cage blushed no one could see it in his rubbery old cheeks, but his eyes showed a shame that had ripened with the years. His eyes made four with Mama King's. They were young people once again, engaged in mortal combat. To each the other had to be conquered and extirpated.

'You digging up a past that was buried half a century ago,' he snarled, see-sawing his knobbly fists in the air. 'I was no more cruel than that ape-man you married. He bumped, bruised and boxed you face and kick you about worse than a football. He was the cruellest, most ignorant man in God's world. His disappearance was the best thing that happened to this town.'

'You lie! You lie!' Mama King yelled, lashing out with two shrunken fists. 'You was after every woman – depending on she and gambling away all she got. Danny never hurt a fly.,

'No need to. He work off his sadistic cruelty half-killing you three times a week,' Ben Le Cage replied tauntingly.

'You yow-yow Missy-man,' Mama King shouted hitting out at him, but he grasped her hands to tightly she screamed. Matron rushed into the room.

'I ain't no Missy-man,' puffed Ben Le Cage. 'Nobody calls me that.'

'Memories! She mustn't have memories. She can't cope with them. I wish I could get them out of her but I can *not*.'

'What you want from me,' Mama King sobbed. 'I told you no tother day. You can never take no for answer.'

Ben Le Cage's eyes looked like nail heads as he muttered, 'I came to see her full of good will. I never know she was mad. Her husband was so ignorant he would kill you for saying tamarind jam does not come from cassava peelings. He hated everything and everybody. Only last night Ginchi and I talked about him. She told me of Mabel's predicament. So I came. I didn't expect to find a crazy old woman dreaming of an imaginary man.'

'What predicament?' snapped Matron, ignoring the rest of his remark. 'This is no predicament here. She in a good home here. You see what we have to contend with? Madness, lunacy, outburst, everything.'

He nodded but did not smile. He walked away as quickly as his two small feet pushed into shiny, patent-leather shoes could carry him; but now and again he glanced behind him just to be certain Mama King had not broken free.

'She was so quiet! So altruistic!' he said sadly. 'What could have brought her to this? Why did they do this to her. As long as she lives, she has to be active. Sitting around made her mad. I hope I never see her again! Thank God I'm leaving tomorrow.' A dark space had come between himself and his village as well as between Mama King and himself. And in that space all the feelings of old age had solidified into a ball of disappointment and rage.

VIII

The incident shattered Mama King. Something inside her had been rubbed raw and sprinkled with salt. Curled up like a foetus she stayed in her room, refusing all food but now and then ripping up her clothes – especially a dark blue dress her daughters had recently sent her.

'Don't tear up that dress Mama King,' pleaded Nurse Tibbs. 'Don't destroy. It bad to destroy. You grandchildren got plenty clothes.'

'I got to get a shirt for Solo and a shirt for Markey, and two ribbon-bows for Cindy.'

'You want food Mama? Eat something! I have a nice sausage here for you.'

'I want two. One for me and one for Danny.'

'Which Danny? This is a woman only place. No Danny allowed!'

Mama King began to cry. 'I want two! I want one for Danny!'

'Don't keep noise!' Matron interrupted sharply. 'I fed up with you and with Danny. At once! Put your teeth in here! Put them in!' She produced a glass of water.

'It not Sunday,' protested Mama King.

'Sunday or not, put them in the glass. Nurse, get the injection ready. We going to have trouble.' Mama King trembled at the word injection.

'You got cold fever already,' said Matron. 'Put them in the glass! You rucktion old woman!'

Mama King plopped her false teeth into the glass. 'I ain't rucktion,' she whined.

'Now give her two big sausages. And she have to eat them … all up. She lucky to get her wish.'

She scurried off to answer the telephone. Mama King bit into the sausage but the thick rubbery skin defied her gums.

The fat congealed in her mouth and she threw the sausages under her bed. The smell attracted Matron's dog. It rushed into the room, dived under the bed, gobbled up the sausages and scurried away to beg for more.

Mama King smouldered. A malignancy came over her wrinkled face and then concentrated itself by the accumulation of infirmity and age, into her eyes. She could easily, had she the necessary weapons, have murdered the matron. But fire was more immediate and how wonderful it would be to set the place afire and laugh loudly and long as the flames annihilated the nasty house!

She sat on her bed playing with thoughts of fire as a child plays with an intricate toy. She hated the dog for eating the sausages and she hated the Matron for giving them to her.

'Mama King,' someone whispered, 'Mabel King, let me in!'

It was Miss Mason.

'I hate injustice. I have got your teeth. I took them out of Matron's glass. She's talking to someone on the telephone – your daughters I believe. She says you are OK. So I took your teeth and dropped Mrs McAbe's in the glass. Mrs McAbe sleeps a lot. I hate this place. It makes me forget and it is unjust. Here you are! You can't be OK without your nice false teeth!'

Mama King snatched her teeth and put them in her mouth.

'Don't you think I am the Scarlet Pimpernel?' asked Miss Mason. 'Matron is wrong-sided most of the time. She has money. I took some. Do you want it?' She gave Mama King two five dollar bills, and as she turned to go she said, 'Keep them in your shoes and don't forget them. They never search your hair though. Hide it in your plait. Pleas', I have no plaits to speak of.'

Mama King examined the bills carefully. She had never found time to look at one closely before. She had never kept one for more than a few minutes, or savoured it or made friends with it. What little came her way had always been a servant of her altruism, her unselfishness and her concern for the needs of others. The feel of money awakened more dormant memories.

'No sooner Token carry her children to America, Cyclette bring her three home. Charlie, Boyson and Markey. Charlie hate everybody even he own self. He no more than eight when he raise his hand to me. I get the axe and threaten to chop it off. That happen to children who knock big people, I tell him. He tremble with fright but he never do it again. Nobody could control Charlie. I didn't want him. I tell his mother come take him. He want a man to bring him up. Trouble follow Charlie like ants follow sugar. He go to Merica and start with the drugs. He give the wrong people the wrong drugs and the right people shoot him. He was seventeen year old. He never taste being a man. Boyson, well he is me fault. I never should treat him normal. Markey, in the Navy they tell me – somewhere in the worl' – all I have is Solo and Cindy. All I want is my family – all together in one room. With me in middle. I slave for them. I work for them and now I here alone, and thin as cigarette paper on this chair in a corner.'

'Mama King,' called Nurse Douglas. 'You OK? What you muttering on about now!'

'Go away you! Stop bawlin' at me.' In a dull monotone she continued.

'I should have take up with Franky. I did like he, but he want me same time as Danny, and he is a passionate man. When he passion raise he could kill! Franky had shop. He was Portuguese-half with a nice smooth face. One night I walk out with he. Was a nice moonlight night. He twist his little finger round me little finger and we walk so quietly and content in the night. I was wishin' for a kiss from him, but he never try. I tell him about Danny.'

'"You love that chop-down man. He chop you down if you cough when he talking. You love that man?"

"What you mean by love? That for white people all that romance. Danny going look after me. I want that kinda man." Little did I know Danny goin' to Aruba, to look for work. When Danny lef' me Franky write to me. One night I left the two girls sleeping and go to the shop.

'"Mabel," he say, "I just want to help you. I don' want nothing from you" – all the time he pushing me on a pile of flour bag. I couldn'. I is a decent woman. I work to buy food for me children than pay for it laying down.'

37

'Ginchi say I stupid. When Tilley hear 'bout it she say "Don't act backward going forward. I think I will try my luck." She end up with plenty salt fish, flour, corn-pork and Junior.'

Unable to comprehend Mama King's persistent talking, Nurse Tibbs had gone down to the laundry-room and brought Carlton to the door of her room.

'I have to tell her two message,' said Carlton. 'Mama Ginchi can' come to see her this Sunday and Markey write. He comin' to see her. He ship in Trinidad and if he get time, he comin'. The message goin' worry her.'

'Tell you what Carlton. Tell her the bad news first, then give her the good news to calm her down.'

'Ver' well,' agreed Carlton.

He knocked.

'I can' sit down, Mama? I got message for you,' he said.

She opened the door.

'Come in quick before they see you.' She gave a furtive glance outside.

'You member Dolly May?'

Mama King nodded.

'Well, no matter! She get baby and Mama Ginchi gone to help wash beddin.' She can' come see you Sunday like she always do.'

Mama King's face fell.

'Even Ginchi forget 'bout me! Even Ginchi gone from me. Carlton I ole and lonely.'

'She ain' turn, and is only one week. But Markey say he comin' to see you. He got ship in Trinidad. And he comin' in a hurry to see you. You remember he and me was bes' friend. That's why he write.'

She smiled broadly and yet her eyes glistened with tears.

'Markey tell you that! I can't remember Markey face. He is the only one lef' of Cyclette children. Boyson dead, then Charlie get shoot and she lef' with Markey. God know everything.'

Carlton put on his cap.

'You goin' Carlton,' Mama King said. 'Walk good, Boy.

Watch where you walkin'! Plenty snake hidin' in the grass.'

She wandered over to the window. It had come alive again. Nurse Douglas stood talking to a young man around her own age. All of a sudden he took her in his arms and kissed her. Mama King started to laugh. 'Aye,' she said, 'life like a liver and man kissing her.' But Nurse Douglas was inside giggling, and talking excitedly to the small group around her.

'You hear the news, Mama?' said Nurse Carey. 'Nurse Douglas getting married! Her man get divorce at last.'

'What about you?' Mama King said.

'I correspond with a boy that went to America. He was fourteen. I was twelve. We still write. He studying to be a eye-doctor. He has to be a doctor first. I must wait and see. He meeting very much nicer girls every day.'

'Well, married is easy – livin' together is hard. Take you time. I got two grandson in America.'

'I know,' said Nurse Carey. She resisted the temptation to say more.

Mama King held her stomach and groaned.

'What you groaning for Mama King,' the nurse asked gently. 'You got pain? Something hurting you?' She spoke loudly as nurses usually speak to the sick, and as most people speak to the old.

'I got pain – all over,' Mama King replied. 'Inside and out. I feel pain everywhere. Livin' together is very hard. like it was for me and Danny.'

'Never mind, Mama King, one day it will end. One way or another it will.'

'Think about the party tomorrow. You going?' Mama King did not reply.

IX

It was Miss Mason's birthday. 'June 28 in the year of our Lord, far into time,' said Matron with a chuckle.

'How old am I?' Miss Mason asked like a sheepish child. 'Am I a hundred yet?' Her pragmatism had begun to tarnish suddenly.

'No. Ninety. You quite active for your age. And you inquisitive too.' Matron was in a good mood.

'Why is it my birthday?' asked Miss Mason. 'I don't want birthdays. I want to die but I can't. I only sleep.'

'Because God let you live another year.'

'Why?'

'Because God is the Good Shepherd and we is the sheep,' said Agnes.

Quietly Miss Mason pressed the palms of her hands together and said:

'When I lay me down to sleep
I give the Lord my soul to keep
If I die before I wake
I pray the Lord my soul to take.'

She stood still – everything about her quiet – her eyes shining, but only like dead fish at night.

'Give me my party dress,' she demanded on impulse. 'The green one with the sequins on the hem. That is my party dress. I always wear that dress when I go out.' With difficulty she put it on.

'Now give me my party.' She put on her battered cloche hat.

'Not till t'ree o'clock! You must wait,' said Nurse Douglas. 'Rest yourself. You got to serve out the tea. It's your birthday, you know.' Miss Mason slipped her comforter in her mouth, cuddled her doll and climbed into her bed.

'Is the excitement,' said Matron. 'We shouldn' have put up the decorations so soon. Is all the flowers. Old people can' take

40

too much strain.'

While Miss Mason slept, the others dressed themselves. Some wore clean bed-jackets, some day dresses, some fancy housecoats. Mama King was content to look out of her window. No amount of coaxing or talking could get her out of her room. She could hear the women shakily singing 'It's a long way to Tipperary,' 'Show me the way to go home' and 'Goodnight ladies.' For an instant, she poked her head round the door to admire the lily-white tablecloth, the flowers and the balloons.

When all was ready, they woke Miss Mason. She sat up while they sang 'Happy Birthday', but she seemed tired and lay down again. Tea was served and then ice-cream and cake while Miss Mason snored.

'Get her up to drink her health,' ordered Matron. 'You do it Nurse Douglas. Agnes too rough.'

Nurse Douglas sat on the bed and called quietly: 'Miss Mason. Time for grog! Sit up and drink you health! Happy Birthday.'

Miss Mason's snoring stopped as if some one had snipped it with sharp scissors. She gave a brief, hissing sound.

'Miss Mason!…Miss Mason!' The urgency in Nurse Douglas' voice brought Matron to the bedside.

'Oh God,' whispered Nurse Douglas, 'She gone.'

'Gone where?' asked Matron. 'All this trouble and she ain' even taste the cake! Don't say more. Wheel out the bed! Don't excite dem! Tell dem she is a little sick.'

They quickly wheeled out the bed. Nurse Tibbs played 'Hide the parcel' with different women guessing where she had hidden it. They were all enjoying themselves so much they forgot why Miss Mason had been wheeled out, and ignored Matron when she told them that Miss Mason had gone to God, and Mrs Gomez was going to take her place next week. After the women were settled, Matron made the usual telephone calls and early the next day Miss Mason's friends, acting for distant relations, took her body away for burial.

That night Mama King ate supper.

'My spirit light as feather. Two good things happen. Marie Mason in heaven at last, and Markey comin' to take me home. I wonder what work they will give me to do.'

The job she disliked most was breaking bricks to repair the furrows in the road. She had to work as a brick-breaker once. There was no choice. It was either that or starvation. There had been a Post Office strike and no letters had been delivered for two months and she could get no wages from America. 'No send-home money. No nothin,' she mumbled as she relived the time.

They paid a shilling a barrel and women sat beside the road every day of the week breaking the bricks with heavy hammers. On Fridays the overseer measured the quantities by the barrel and paid accordingly. Token and Cyclette helped her. They brought the rocks close so that she could reach them easily. At knock-off time they went home dusty outside and 'talking like craupaud before rain come down,' with the dust inside their throats.

One day carelessness came between her hand and a king-size brick. *'Me hand swell up like a balloon. They take me to hospital for injection. All night pain working in the whole hand like bellow. I frighten they cut off me hand. I tell the children Mama goin' get one hand when the doctor cut it off. They start a cry. Mama, Token say, I will be a doctor and put it back. Token was a good name for that child. Ginchi come, she make cochineal poltice and put it on me hand. The next day, the swelling gone down and the pain ease off. I couldn' work no more. I hate breaking brick. I hate that work! I glad I never do it nowadays. But nowadays things never that bad. Tomorrow when Markey come he will get some ointment. I don't have no where to put it but it good to keep in case somebody want. I better go to bed quick and sleep before Markey come. I must look fresh for Markey.*

'Goodnight ladies I turning in! Markey coming to carry me home.'

'Mama King it's only five o'clock,' said Nurse Carey. 'it's too soon to go to bed.'

She pressed her face into her pillow, still talking about Markey.

42

'Hope he walk proud and don't take advantage of women. I hope he father bad blood ain't showing. He father used to beat poor Cyclette like she was a kettle drum. Hm,' she sighed, 'I thinking too much. Thinking will choke me.' But more thoughts of Markey swamped her.

'I hope he is a good, good man. I gave them me own hard-wearing spirit every time I talk to them, every time I dress them, every time I feed then when they was here wid me.'

'I remember the day he win prize in school. I feel so proud. He ain't got mother or father to see him only me. "I bow good, Mama?" he axe me, "when I get me prize?" Then two month pass and he mother say pack that boy up and send him to me. I want him now. They cry. So I say, "But they don't know you. Me is they mother?"'

'Cyclette start accusing me. "You never show them me photo. You never say this is your mother." Oh Lord give me faith – give me faith.'

Accompanied by her gramophone, Matron sang briefly, and then made her rounds. She went from bed to bed, her eyes moving over the captured women like a torch. She saw not only them – single and isolated – but all their physical progenitors that the beds had served. Their distorted faces, their decrepitude, their dependency, their illness, their senescence, their odours; all leered at her from the eyes of those who now lay there.

The rain drummed down self-indulgently and lightning magically translated the growls of thunder for all to read. Each flash showed Matron a face she had known and served. To Mama King each flash showed the faces of the children she had loved and served.

Will Markey come? Will he? The question eddying in her mind subdued her but kept on turning. It could find no resting place. Together they must wander until the hour of truth. Her longing for Markey's coming was absolute and her feelings about her life darted about at one moment, but at another changed into blocks of wood and stone and weighed her down and down into a pit of despair. At each sunset she scratched the wall to mark the days. There were five little scratches and five days had come and gone.

As the days passed, thoughts of Markey's impending visit overwhelmed her. Her heart took turns to spin like a top in anticipation, or to sink into the abyss where all the disappointments of her life lay dead or dying.

In their effort to obliterate all traces of Miss Mason, the nurses rushed around, tenaciously pursuing the rites of reconstruction and extermination. The mattress on which the old lady had slept, allowed at last to reveal a gaping sore of brown straw, was being replaced, and just for a moment the smell of urine resurrected her.

Her doll, her comforter and the clothes she wore with so much pride, found place beside a heap of sodden paper, and at the sight of them, those who felt fellowship with her, heard once again her chirruping voice as she unselfconsciously took liberties with everyone and her cackling laughter when she was caught out.

Nurse Agnes deftly rummaged through a box of letters, and read with sniggering incomprehension, a poem Miss Mason had once written to some imagined lover:

'I stand enraptured, yet afraid
To follow or to start.
Your love, beloved one,
Beams its light to sear my heart.'

As if on cue, Mrs Gomez the replacement entered the room. She must have been tall in her youth but stooped in her old age as if to accommodate an invisible rucksack on her narrow back. She took quick, stealthy glances at everything, allowing her eyes a wink or two when noting what must be grumbled about in the future. Yet, her eyes were so shallow they seemed in danger of falling out of their sockets. Every few minutes or so, she sniffed like a forest animal that tracked its prey by scent. The veins on her neck were like strong thick cord, and when she unashamedly changed from her street clothes into a lively green and white dress, her breasts swung about like a pair of dark brown socks in the washday wind. Cheerfully she sat herself on her bed and from a pretty box began eating what seemed to be chocolates.

The nurses were aghast but dared not intervene – not on her first day, and within the hour of admission. 'People do strange things when they feel strange,' whispered Nurse Tibbs. 'Let her eat till she stop.'

Before Nurse Douglas could reply Mrs Gomez said, 'Don' susu 'bout me. You tell me. I tell you. Don' susu. Didn' your mother learn you dat? Backru grow you up?'

At the same moment Mama King emerged from her room. She looked troubled.

'I can't remember Markey face,' she said. 'All I member is a boy. They put me here. Come find you grandmother! Don't leave your grandmother here.'

She repeated those words again and again, like a child rolling a marble in a jar.

Miss Turvey laughed, a cold freezing laugh. 'The bus break down! The wheel come off! The driver dead! You grandson ain' comin! Ha ha-ha-ha-ha-ha-ha!'

Mama King could not hold back her tears. She ran into her room and banged the door shut. But she could not keep out Miss Turvey's voice.

Matron turned on Turvey shouting, 'Order! None of your slackness and common-class behaviour. You act like you didn' get home-training.' When they were quiet she continued: 'This is Mrs Gomez. Ida Gomez. I want you all to get to know her and give her affection.' She pointed to Mrs Gomez like a policeman guiding traffic.

Mrs Gomez smiled. Only then did she share her chocolates with those closest to her. She ignored Miss Turvey's piercing cries of 'Gie me one! Gie me two. Gie me t'ree.'

Matron did not stay in the room. She scurried to her office. But Nurse Tibbs timidly knocked on Mama King's door and said, 'Mama King, a young man telephone. Name of Markey. He coming to see you. Big taxi.'

'I know,' she replied, 'Ginchi and Carlton tell me. He is my grandson. I want see him and I don't want see him.'

'Well, that's up to you. I did what Matron say. I told you.'

The women settled down. Mrs Gomez paced the room

trying to make friends with her new environment. Then she walked to the window at the far corner of the room and stared at the world as if seeing for the last time all that was familiar and friendly and known.

At about five thirty, Matron returned to the hall accompanied by a young man dressed in a sailor's uniform. He was six foot tall, broad-shouldered and confident in step and action. His uniform emphasised his physical proportions, the openness of his face, and his ready, eloquent smile. She introduced him to each member of staff and added that he had flown in from his base in the Caribbean just to see his grandmother. He added, 'I have a forty-eight hour pass. I can just make this visit from Trinidad. It is indeed a flying visit. Can I see my grandmom please? My God! How time flies! I was thirteen when I last saw her. May I see her?' There was a mixture of agitation and sorrow in his voice.

'Just talking about the years gives them impossible dimensions and significance,' he said.

They opened the door. She was still in bed but wrapped like a corpse in her sheet. Her body was neither straight nor rigid. It made an irregular shape in the middle of the bed, while the materials she had cut up, and thrown around, seemed like creatures from another place.

'Mama! This is Markey. I've come to see you – to bring you love from all the family.' Nothing happened.

'Mama!' Markey said again. His voice touched her senses this time and she scrambled out of the bed – her pepper and salt hair unkempt, her eyes wide with astonishment, her body gaunt and wasted under a washed-out night-gown gave her a ghostly look. Markey swallowed the lump in his throat once, twice, thrice, but each time it returned and had grown larger. The sight of her overwhelmed him. He remembered her dark-haired and strong, able to get the stopper from a bottle with her teeth. She was purposeful and positive. Now here she was, a haunted ghost with a haunting past. The family had imagined her happy, interminably giving and caring and sharing in friendship and community. Never getting older.

Immortal. What had the years done to her? True she had been ill. But this was more than illness. She was old, but age did not enhance or dignify her. What had they done to her?

'Markey,' she said at last 'You didn' forget me. Them throw me out like rubbish. Token, Cyclette, Cindy and Solo. I work for all of you. Now I here alone. Take me home Markey. In you big, big ship.'

'I bring you love from all the family,' he said. 'We talk about you. We pray for you. We have so much love for you, you should feel it enclosing you all the way out here.'

'Nobody know if I sad, or hungry, or alone. I slave for all of you. You all go away leave a wound that fester more and more. Is easy to love from a distance – with the wide ocean between.'

She had her head on his shoulder now. There was no weight to her. No one could call her a burden. She was so light, he could pick her up in his arms like a baby.

'Mama,' he said brightly, 'I promise to do something to change your situation. You don't need all this looking after. You need more self-actualisation. You don't want a seat among the dead-beats. You are being pushed right along to the graveyard. Seeing you like this has been a hell of an experience for me!'

He was silent for a long time, watching her twisting her material into incomprehensible shapes, and as if to accompany the flow of feelings, the rain beat a weird rhythm on the roof top.

'Markey,' Mama King said, 'you tall and you strong. I glad you come. I glad I live to see you.'

'Momma, Aunty Token, Solo and Cindy will all be glad I've seen you. They'll get news at first hand. Now I must see Miss Ginchi and Carlton then I'll be off to board my ship.'

Miss Ginchi stood waiting, the half-opened door behind her. It blew hard brushing her clothes against her frail body to show how thin she too had become. Markey remembered the bijou house clearly and when he was quite close to her, bit by bit the familiar face returned. Her eyes were the same deep brown, and her aquiline nose seemed to have taken over her narrow overboned face.

She hugged Markey and said, 'Tell me my boy, tell me all.'

'I never expected to see her that way. I remember her young – not fumbling like a helpless screwball. Not nuts! What have they done to her?'

'Confinement and do-nothing destroy people. She like to hustle. She hustle all her life,' replied Miss Ginchi. 'When she don't do it, her body is deprive. She write a letter to Token the other day! Read it. I never send it. I didn't want to worry Token.'

Markey ran his eyes over the few lines.

'That's the cry of a desperate woman,' he said. 'I will tell my momma as soon as I get back home – although that won't be for some time. We're en route to South America, then we will go to Korea and then on to Israel.'

'Miss Ginchi,' he said pressing a twenty dollar bill into her hand. 'Tell her I love her. Look after her for me. Keep this for yourself. I'll try to come back soon. My grandmother is on a journey to limbo.'

'Ah,' she replied shaking her head. 'Fara-fara make ochro dry on tree.'

X

The rain had stopped, and the puddles reflected the light from the open windows. A mere slither of a moon peered out into the damp, blue-black night. A donkey brayed enthusiastically and an owl hooted in the distance. The night vendors, selling roasted peanuts, black-pudding, Souse and Channa were preparing their stalls. Nostalgia hit Markey like a brick.

'Stop, here,' he said to the driver of his taxi. 'I'll try some souse. I used to love this stuff.'

He had not eaten it for fourteen years but it brought back the pleasures, longings and terrors of his childhood, and the presence of his grandmother. She was always there – like a rock – like a haven in a storm. His mother, trusting her completely, left him there without so much as a backward glance; and he had found not only care and concern but commitment, courage and compassion. Now they had left her to strangers as a reward for all she had done. They had let her down! He broke into uncontrollable sobbing.

'Somebody dead, sir?' asked the taxi-driver hesitantly. 'You crying like if your mother die.'

'Yes, well no, several things are dead – memory, a spirit, a time – a place. I guess all that goes to make up a person.' They sped on and outwards in the direction of the airport. 'I went to that home to see my grandmom. Guess I just couldn't take the change in her. Good people die of old age – in a Rest Home. Uncle Abel never came home.'

'The same person never returns to the same place. You never find the same people – all you find is old people with familiar voices. Voices never change,' replied the driver.

'Would she be there in another year? That place is destructive – she might as well be dead. My poor mother! My poor grandmother! Who is fading her out?'

A solitary flower seller, determined to dispose of the last few

49

bunches, nonchalantly urged travellers to 'Take a bunch home for the wifey.' Markey bought several bunches. 'Take these to the Eventide Home I just left. Say they are for my grandmother. It's best to send flowers to the living. Here is the money.' The quantity of both surprised the driver!

'You're a feeling man,' the taxi-driver said. 'A rare, feeling man. Where would we be without our grandmothers when work takes our mothers from us. They like the backbone in the fish and the thickening in the soup.'

'See you,' said Markey. 'See you in church.'

And he was gone.

The next day the fetid smell of wilting flowers caused Mama King's broad sensitive nose to tingle a little.

'You would think I dead already, Markey sending me all dese half-dead flowers,' she said walking around and emphasising their poignancy by touching them almost sacramentally.

Nurse Tibbs teased, 'Roses are red, Violets are blue, Markey loves you and me too.'

Mama King chuckled. There was a sudden rejuvenation – a resurgence of spirit in her voice and she tantalisingly replied:

'He comin' back for me! He busy about the world! Workin'. But he will come back for me! He promise me!'

She stared out of her window hoping that she would see him striding towards her but there was only the day out there, sparkling as if it had been sprayed with silver. The air fresh and earth-scented after the rain drew the birds to it, compelling them to sing in celebration.

Visitors who came during morning-time on Sundays dribbled in and as she matched indifferent visitors to eagerly waiting old women, she whispered prayerfully:

'Markey you promise. You promise to come for me! You mus' come Markey. You got to come.'

With each word the germ of strength lying deep inside her took root and rapidly grew into a towering plant, rejecting her feeling of anxiety and abandonment. For a moment the exact nature of her problem flashed like a spotlight on a stage and then vanished. She stared around the room until a piece of material, snakelike and sinister, drew her eyes. She seized it and stroked it, all the while assuring herself that her sit-and-stare existence would one day end.

As the days passed, she grew quiet, almost contemplative. She changed from confrontation to co-operation. The nurses noticed and praised her. She was accepting and helpful. The soliloquising and anger had given way to quiet resolution.

'Mama King,' said Nurse Douglas. 'You t'row way you long spoon? You not stirring up t'ings dese days!'

Fewer drugs were used to control the protestors. The women laughed more and worried less. Sunshine entered the home through deeds and actions. Mama King was happier but her resolve to escape never wavered.

'It is strange,' observed the Matron, 'what the sight of a single member of a family do for Mama King. All old people want is to be remembered. They prefer their own people. And so they should. Family include old and young.' Matron spoke correctly and calmly. She too was more relaxed.

By now Mama King had made a friend of Mrs Gomez and listened again and again to her life-story.

'My children dead, you know. All of dem. I carry dem full term and when they born, they dead. All five of dem.'

'Eh heh!' said Mama King. 'Heavy cross to bear!'

'Only my nephew I got. He is lawyer. He lookin' after the money side! Life is funny. You born! You live and you die! One of my fits will kill me,' Mrs Gomez spoke in a steady unemotional way.

'You does get fits?' asked Mama King, barely concealing her curiosity.

'Yes. You sound like you grudgeful. Wha' you didn' get don' hanker after. My fits is me lot but not children!'

Mama King gloomily replied, 'I hate anybody that take children from their mother. Even God. You is a brave woman! I en brave like you.'

'Why you eyes always fix on the door?' asked Mrs Gomez. 'You always watchin' the door.'

'Matron say I could walk free,' replied Mama King. 'That's why. You say you does get fits?'

'Yes, they come on me like a t'ief. I don' know they comin'.'

'If you get one on Friday when beggars come, they will carry it away. Friday is a holy day! They call Friday, Good Friday. Beggars take sickness away!'

'For true?' asked Mrs Gomez – her religion beginning to come alight. 'Which Friday?'

'Any Friday. When de beggars come. Any Friday.'

'Good Lord, help me! If she get fits, while they goin on wid she, I can run way and fin' Markey. Lord, she want to see your face and I want to see me grandson face. Lord help me!'

She walked freely out into the grounds, making sure not to offend while she waited for her Friday to come. She would then grasp Markey's hand and they would run away and hide where Matron would never find them. She sneezed as a young child would, and then she smelt him close-homely as ripening fruit, familiarly her own.

Even across the deep chasm of her past she could hear her younger self saying, *'Change you shirt, Markey. Change! You smell like you been chopping wood since early day-dawn, clean clothes on the tray over yonder, change you shirt. You mustn' be poor, black and dirty.'*

She usually returned paid-for washing in the tray perched comfortably on her head each Friday, but on other days it was the show-case for the grandchildren's clothes washed and ironed with love.

'"Change you' shirt, Markey." He was the last to go. The last baby I ever get. He always walk close to on he long, man-man legs, a melon-cut grin on he face, he small, white shining teeth and he eyes brown as almond and he skin so nice and smooth like sand. But sometimes he run from me, and I have to shout '"Markey, you bumptious boy, passing me like you don' know me! I still you grandmother! You shame to own me! You forget how good I was to you every day of you' life. You born a hot raining Tuesday. Bup! You drop on the floor. You bawl like duppee choir-boy. Me hand was the first that touch you!"'

She chuckled softly, and in her imagination walked until she reached the pond. The water hardly stirred but some dragonflies hunted close to the surface. From the depths of the pond she could hear voices of women long dead and gone – the washerwomen she used to know, singing as they beat the dirt from the clothes with their faithful wooden beaters. They had left the echoes of their songs to tell how life had robbed them of their youth, of their spirit and then of their lives.

The squelching of cheap soap, and the slithering confidence of the starch, the familiar feel of cotton, crisp as new biscuit, were all beneath her fingers. Where would all the family be without her efforts? She scratched her head, perplexed. *'How many did I cook for? Five or four or three. I doan know "I doan know where all this forgetfullness come from. It make me fret. Markey like to eat. Call anything food and it ready for Markey teeth."'*

XI

When it rained her spirits fell and she could do nothing but stand and stare, depression hanging over her like a cloud. And there was Matron shouting as if her voice had been starched and left in the sun to harden!

'Marma King! Do something! Be something,' she would say. 'Think something! Don't stand there with a empty bucket for a mind.'

'Matron why you lock me up when Cindy married? I never go to the wedding!' she asked after a bout of shouting and in a state of confusion.

'Oh Marma King, I sorry! You never tell me the date.'

Matron had sensed her confusion especially when she began hanging the flowers she had carefully dried about the room. Thoughts of her family rolled around in her head, like waves, and gave her courage to add, 'You so wicked Matron! Wicked, wicked, wicked! I know it, and I say it.'

Matron sucked her teeth and gave her dog a biscuit.

'Marma King,' she said. 'If you want to think that, think that!'

Mama King laughed and said, 'You think you nice to look at but you not. You is a fat, voluptuous woman. Nobody want you! That's why you here fighting old people. One eye man is king in blind eye man country. You backside bigger than Mr Johnson car.' Mama King had said all she intended to say, a silence descended on everyone as it did when the women quarrelled with Matron or anyone else. Mama King stared out of her window. She could see herself as a young woman waiting to beg a ride in the donkey cart. She felt angry when the donkey cart changed into the bed in which she slept. She thought once more of the futility of her life.

'I am going lazy-handed to meet my Maker. Me mother dead with sod in her hair. Me father dead with rice grass underneath him. And me I

sittin' till me bones get sore waitin.'

She stared at her hands and at once recalled a game she played with her grandchildren when they were sick.

'Grandmother, grandmother I am sick.
Send for the doctor quick, quick, quick.
Doctor, doctor I will die?
How many people going to cry?'

Then they would count and crack their fingers to sound like walking feet. She hugged herself as she hugged them after they had counted to ten all those years ago.

Miss Ginchi and Carlton walked in and all three laughed at her actions. 'I see you huggin' and kissin' yourself, Mabel,' Miss Ginchi remarked lightheartedly.

'It's because Markey come. He comin' back, you know. If he don' fine me, I will fine he. I goin' out of dis place. This is one graveyard I don' want, so help me! You see Markey? He look nice?'

Miss Ginchi nodded. 'Don't do nothing stupid, Mabel,' she pleaded. 'Don't act childish. Tell me what you goin' do.' Miss Ginchi rose to go.

Mama King smiled. She had visualised a way out of Frangipani House. She would go on a suitable Friday.

'I en talking. I en telling anybody nothin' I goin' do. If I tell you, you tell another body. That en make two, you know. It make 11.' She drew two harsh lines in her palm with a bony finger.

Each day she thought of new ways to escape. Should she ask Carlton about his bicycle? She had not forgotten how to ride. She rode five miles to see her cousin Quango – the blacksmith. His face which seemed to stretch down into his chest came vividly to her, and there they were, the beads of glistening sweat on his brow. And then his squared gleaming white teeth. Yes, she could ride a bike as she once did to visit Quango. But perhaps she could walk by night and hide by day! Had the roads changed since her imprisonment in this home? Dreary doubts filled her head and caused her to abandon the plans which brought so much dread and so much heartache. She decided to let the day name itself.

Talking to Mrs Gomez had eased her mind but now she no longer could. Was it last week she had found Mrs Gomez, face contorted, limbs jerking in a frenzy and froth coming from her mouth like soapy water on wash day? She could not now remember the day. But Mrs Gomez had soiled herself. The smell came over the place like rain. Nurse Tibbs had said that Mrs Gomez had taken a stroke. There was nothing to do but wait and wonder. Would Mrs Gomez die soon after or suffer for her sins and waste away? Would the plans to escape take root and grow? Would she find Markey? She had many questions but only a few sure answers.

In fact, Mrs Gomez was now bedridden and speechless from the stroke. She had become a vegetable, her bed a patch that was tended if there was time.

XII

Mama King's Friday came at last. She put on two dresses one on top of the other, ate a scant breakfast and then told Nurse Douglas that her mouth tasted bitter. She wanted, she said, sweet-sage tea to cure the biliousness which was indicated by the bitter taste.

'I see sweet-sage growing just past them croton bush by the big tree!' She pointed in the direction of the tree.

'When you see sweet-sage?' asked Nurse Douglas with some dubiety.

'Long,' said Mama King, 'Long time. One of these days when I can walk out I goin' pick some. When Ginchi come next week perhaps.'

'Perhaps,' replied Nurse Douglas and hurried off to answer the telephone, see to Mrs Gomez and do a thousand other things.

As soon as she disappeared, Mama King, her heart throbbing and prayerful, skipped out of the door and headed for the latrine. Though it stank like a duppee's oven, she slipped inside and stooped close to the floor. She listened. Only the gurgling of bilgy water and putrefying matter could be heard. She looked up. Above her head a family of bats roosted and above them, the holes in the corrugated-iron roof showed the sky a lucid blue. Her hands crept along the walls, felt their age-old dustiness, and froze! What if walls should fall down like the walls of Jericho? What if God should expose her and make a Jonah of her? She slipped off the blue dress, and exposed the dark green one. The beggars were now approaching. She could hear the scrape, trudge and clatter of their feet, the dull structural chanting of the men, and the plaintive shrieking of the women. Children indifferently echoed whichever melody they chose.

'Give us to eat! Give us food! We are the poor! God give you more!'

There was a disorientating quality about their chanting which at that time of day compelled response.

'We are poor! Give us alms! Let us eat!' They cried out again.

At this point Mama King dropped her blue dress into the pit and watched it disappear. Matron always waited until the beggars huddled in a sheepish wondering mass, before ceremonially opening the door and approaching with the sacrement of her charity, which she enumerated in a voice as cold and distant as her uniform from their clothes.

'A little raw rice, money in small silver, a cup or two of sugar and oil – a little oil'. After their obsequious acceptance she would stand statue-still, her short fat hands hanging in front of her smooth blue uniform, her stubby fingers intertwined to await their blessing which came from a single voice. Then turning on her heels, she would take the same number of steps back into the house, while the children chorused their thanks.

'Tenky Matron Ma'am. Tenky ole peopul dem. Tenky nurse-dem ma'am.'

They were leaving now. Would they pass her way? Would a nurse dawdle by the window? Her heart was a tremulous as a leaf in the wind. They took the curve that brought them close. A child lifting her ragged dress entered the latrine. She suppressed a scream on seeing Mama King. The women came and peeped at her questioningly. She followed them out, gesturing, supplicating, trying to communicate her one bursting desire and her only overwhelming need. Instinctively they understood and encircling her, they led her away. Only a slight softening of their voices showed their surprise but their disciplined striding helped her away. Her feet trembled beneath her and the dry heat from the road shot through them like darts. Yet desire gave her courage and she trudged on. In the end, however, the heat became her master. She leaned against a tree and in its shade found a coolness which refreshed her. Then suddenly there was movement in the distance. Were they being chased?

But the children shouted joyously at the old man who walked past them after some time. He was the donkey-man – the man who impounded stray donkeys, and kept fruit and biscuits in the depths of his pocket. He did not notice Mama King. A bird came close to catch the big winged flies floating about in the ageing day and he blessed it and walked on.

'Who is boss man?' Mama King asked in her effort to understand things.

'Me!' replied Pandit Prem who had thanked Matron.

'I got to meet up with me grandson! He looking for me too. Matron don't want me! Keep me!'

'Wha' if policeman come?'

'None will come. I ent belong to nobody. I jus' ole. Nobody care 'bout ole.'

'We keep you! But if police come we leave you. We hide.'

The children watched and listened and then wandered over the grass touching a leaf, a tree, a flower, and smiling softly. The little circumstances of their daily lives were enough for them and they played with the sticks, stones and all nature's bric-a-brac that lay about them.

They were far from Frangipani House now. A prayer of thanks welled up from inside Mama King to match the tears in her eyes. She slowly stooped and gathered a handful of grass and pressed it to her heart.

By nightfall they were outside the town. They led her to a bothy which the road-builders had abandoned. The walls were made of wooden slats and the floor cold underfoot, and smelling of cow-dung. She shared the money among them and lay down on some straw. Sumintra, a small, busy, smiling woman with rotten front teeth brought her a bowl of thin soup and she drank it gratefully.

'Give me shoes,' Sumintra said nonchalantly. Mama King slipped her feet out of them and pushed them over.

Sumintra skilfully aimed and threw them out. They dropped into a stream which the old woman was yet to discover.

'You beggar now!' Sumintra muttered, and then sat down

beside her.

'Who you belong?' Sumintra asked.

'Nobody,' Mama King replied. 'Me picknie cross big water.'

One by one they came and sat in a protective ring around her showing her the marks left by stones thrown at them, or by dogs that had been set upon them. 'Hot cigarettes worse.' explained Sumintra. 'Hot cigarette very worse.'

Mama King was never more moved to contentment and happiness. One of the little girls approached her and curled up in her lap. And then drop by drop her mothering feeling returned to her. She slept well that night.

XIII

She woke early to hear the little birds breathlessly singing. Some flitted over the grass seeking food for their young. And then she felt the sun in all its glory, a gentle breeze and the green grass beneath her shoeless feet. She sang for the first time in years.

She looked up and down the little lane beside the bothy. Markey was nowhere to be seen. She ate little but Sumintra urged her to eat more. She fumbled with her spectacles, and deciding that she no longer needed them threw them on the bed of straw.

Suddenly one of the men shouted, 'Hide she! Hide she! Policeman ah come.'

Motioning Mama King to lie down, they piled some jute bags over her, walked outside and waited for the young policeman to approach.

'Mornin' sergeant,' Pandit Prem greeted him. 'Wha' you want?'

'You see one old lady stray about? She walk slow and she got blue dress – black – blue.'

'No, sergeant! You want look inside to make sure. It twel' of we and six children, want we count them. You don't care if we call you sergeant?'

'No Pandit but if you see one old lady, come to the station and tell me.'

'Yes sergeant! We go tell you.'

One of the children appeared wearing the spectacles and everyone, even the policeman grinned. They watched him till he was out of sight. Then they laughed in a sly, subdued manner while they freed Mama King and finally gave her access to the unstirring contentedness of their lives.

In a shawl that covered her head, she accompanied them on their expeditions hoping to meet her grandson, but days

passed and he did not come. She felt faint with disappointment. Where was Markey? Had he forgotten her?

On some days she remained in the bothy with the children
and hoped that he would find her there. She thought of the
home too. Had Mrs Gomez gone to her maker. Nurse Carey,
what about her? The cycle of expectation and disappointment
burnt great holes in her mind, confusing and depressing her.
Doubt surrounded her like a shroud. She walked beside the
stream, shallow, half submerging bits of wood and reflecting
the sunshine. Suddenly there was Markey striding towards
her. She ran towards him, with outspread arms, but they
stayed empty. Markey had gone. She must now be content to
hope that he would find her one day soon.

Pandit and his band protected her and cared for her, and
built insight and understanding into her new life.

There is something about the old that releases the desire in
younger people, whatever their station in life, to protect them
and share with them. So Pandit consoled her and kept her
spirits fresh and resolute.

'Your grandson comin!' said Pandit, 'I know he comin! He
never turn he back on you. He will come and put end together
for you.'

Memories of her previous life receded and she settled down
into the routine rhythms of the beggars' existence. On Fridays
she stayed in the bothy – not daring to visit Frangipani House.
Matron, Pandit said, gave him funny looks in her attempt to
decide if he and his group had something to do with the old
lady's disappearance.

Three weeks later, Matron confronted him and asked him:
'You see a old lady walking at Fowl Corner?'

'Plenty lady walk at Fowl Corner. Beggar lady. Plenty,
plenty!'

'Not beggar. She got blue dress!'

Pandit smiled and nodded. His manner was so obsequious,
Matron assumed he would never dare lie to her.

At first everyone regarded Mama King's disappearance as
a prank, then as a slight aberration on her part, and then as

the beginning of a tragedy with police and reporters snooping round. Jack Roper was the reporter Matron feared most and visions of his bulging eyes in a hawkish face made her tremble.

She moved about the home with more ill-will than usual – fussing and carping, while feelings of guilt, flitted around her head like persistent flies.

'What I going to do?' she snapped into the air. 'What I going to tell she family when they descend on me?' Then she would raise her voice another octave and ask, 'What if they find her dead? They will never forgive me. I got to ask Bubble Elder to help me find her.'

Bubble Elder was the police sergeant who loved doing favours, especially for vulnerable women. He had earned his nickname 'Bubble' because, a voluble talker, he was often to be seen in full flow, a rim of froth bubbling round his mouth.

From time to time he came to the home, sparing Olga inquests for suspicious deaths. While giggling suggestively he would tell her what lovely light-brown skin she had. She dangled her love just beyond his reach and always kept him striving for it, but he showed little interest besides physical admiration for her.

She telephoned him, and he came promptly. They were closeted together for some hours but at last they emerged, she looking extremely relaxed, and buoyed up by his promises to find Mama King in a day or two. She resumed her work with an increased sense of power. But Mama King did not return and she was not found and the 'shout and search' continued.

Miss Ginchi fainted at the news and was only resuscitated when someone borrowed some smelling salts from a neighbour, six houses away. Nurse Douglas and Nurse Tibbs tearfully agreed, 'We really like Mama King. Sometimes she is a bit of a handful but we really like her. She is a nice, clean lady. She don't pass water anywhere but where she should. Poor old lady.' Carlton had his own theory: 'The Martians come down and taken her to No-Where Land in a spaceship.' But Mama King's disappearance was becoming stale news. Nobody had found a dead body and the search for her was running out of steam.

What Matron feared most was that the old woman's body, decaying and done-for, would be discovered at a time when it was inconvenient for her community status.

Sadly she recalled her poor Uncle Zekie who never wanted anything out of life but small pocketfuls of diamonds and a little box of gold.

'But what did poor Uncle Zekie get? Nothing. What happen to poor Uncle Zekie? He lose his way in the deep, dark bush.' She turned on the tap letting the water flow over her hands.

She shook her head as she reconstructed the memory. They found him emaciated and half-dead, flies and bugs getting drunk on his worn-out blood.

'His face swell up just like a balloon, and his voice, Lord it terrible. And the voice coming out of a big sore-mouth. Just like a jumbie voice.' She soaped her hands thoroughly. Impetuously she buried her face in her soapy hands, and unwittingly gave the soap-suds access to her eyes. The stinging in her eyes acted like fuel to her anger, and she swore like a drunk on a Saturday night.

With conviction she added: 'We curse. All of us curse! God curse us good and proper!'

Suddenly she was overcome by the certainty of blame, criticism and accusations that would be heaped on her. It frightened her so much, she fell on her knees.

'God,' she said. 'Have Mercy! Have Mercy!'

XIV

Although Mama King ate less well, she felt stronger and the healthy curiosity with which she had been blessed drew her towards the fish market with Sumintra. The fish market was a rough and tumble cluster of stalls, roofed with interwoven coconut-palm fronds to keep out the sun and the rain. Before catching sight of the market one smelt its odours riding the breeze unashamedly. A flock of crows were perpetually resident close by, and quarrelled and squabbled over the entrails of fish that tarnished the sand.

Sumintra quickened her pace and shouted 'Come long! Pandit say quick, quick, we mus come.' Mama King ignored her and bolted through the crowd.

Sumintra headed for the fry-fish shop. At the sight of her the shopkeeper rummaged under a rickety stall, pulled out an oil-stained parcel and gave it to her. Not a word passed between them. She sniffed the parcel, put it into her cloth bag and started out of the market. The old lady was nowhere to be seen. Sumintra rushed round looking for her and at last found her crouching in front of a woman leaning against a low wall. Mama King grasped the woman's hand and pointed and talked for a few minutes and then cupped her hand to receive the shining coins she was being paid. The feel of the money lifted her into the air and carried her back to the days when she earned money to get more and more for her grandchildren.

'I did buy a money-box and a nice pair of lace-up shoes for Charlie. Charlie use to wear out shoes before you say "Sonny come home." As for Cindy and Solo they like book. As fast as they read one you buy another. Markey come, I going buy him something really nice.'

'Ole lady,' said Sumintra, 'Come outa de market, leh we go … This is choke-and-rob place. Babulal give me fish cake.'

They started out. 'I tell fortune,' said Mama King. 'I tell the woman what is in her hand. She give me this. The first time I tell fortune. God forgive me for tellin' lie.'

She showed Sumintra the coins and then quickly closed her hand over them. They walked on until they came to the cake-shop, a lively little place full of noise, cheap cakes and a gaggle of young men standing around, or leaping and dancing to the music. Mama King stood a few yards away and listened too. Some instruments beckoned to her. Others demanded the money, and yet others enticed her into the shop. Mystical voices bade her 'buy a cool iced drink for herself and her friend. Be grateful. Repay kindness with kindness.'

The easy rhythm and complex movements of the young men engaged all her senses and although conscious of her scrutiny, they continued to leap and dance and prance, a few of them mouthing the words of the song overflowing from the sound system inside the shop:

'Grandma's hands clapped in church on Sunday
mornings.
Grandma's hands played the tambourine so well.
Grandma's hands used to issue out a warning,
She'd say Billy don't you run so fast,
Might fall on a piece of glass.
Might be snakes there in that grass.
Grandma's hands.
Grandma's hands sowed the local land with mother.
Grandma's hands used to ache sometimes and swell.
Grandma's hands used to lift her face and tell her.
She'd say "Baby, grandma, understands
That you really love that man."
Put yourself in Jesus' hands.
Grandma's hands.'

Mama King edged past them. She was fearful of the fall she'd take if in their wild manifestation of youthful strength they should bump into her. Suddenly she resolved to buy a large bottle of mauby to share with all her friends, and with her rags flowing in the wind and throwing weird shadows in the sunshine she entered the shop. The sheen on the coins seemed to increase their value, as she placed them confidently down.

'Big bottle, mauby,' she said excitedly. There was a smile broader than that of a contented bride on her face. She felt happy just to be there and to touch and to see.

Two of the lads exchanged glances, broke away from the mass of swaying bodies and followed her out of the shop. They walked round the corner and waited for her to come.

The soothing lilting, compelling rhythm of the song blended with the pot-pourri of instruments in the music and riveted her to the spot. The song was one she had never heard before. For the first time in years she wanted to dance. She tried, but a giggle came instead. The song was about her:

'Grandma's hands used to hand me piece of candy.
Grandma's hands picked me up each time I fell.
Grandma's hands, boy they really came in handy
She say "Mitty don't you whip that boy,
He didn't drop no apple core."
I don't have grandma no more
If I get to heaven I'll look
For Grandma's hands.'

She felt the first crash into her bowels. She keeled over, her head spinning like a wheel. She heard the word 'Beggar' distinctly. From somewhere in her heart a low, tortuous cry of pain hesitatingly surfaced and then voices as if from behind a dark opaque curtain as hands expertly rummaged through her rags.

'She ain't got nothing,' 'That twenty-five was all she got ... we kill she for nothing.' They ran as if a kennel of police dogs were after them. The mauby gurgled out of the bottle and disappeared into the sandy road.

It was a dangerous place for Sumintra. There was blood and she was sure the old woman was dead. The groaning and moaning had stopped. Mama King looked like debris often seen along the shore when the tide was out. Still clutching her bag of fish-cake, Sumintra hurried back into the market and alerted the market constable.

'Come quick. Them boy a choke and rob in broad daylight.

Dis old woman, she dead. Ah road top.' She waved her hands agitatedly and kept on, 'Come quick.' Then she disappeared to alert Pandit and his band.

A crowd of curiosity seekers, newsmongers and sightseers, Carlton among them, followed her. He pushed forward and looked at the bundle lying in the small narrow brickless street.

'Oh me God!' exclaimed Carlton. 'Ah, Mama King! She lost dese four week! She face got blood but ah still know she. She almost me grandmother.'

'Wha she doin' here?' asked the market constable. 'You almost grandmother lost?'

'Me don't know. Me come to buy fish. They send me from Frangipani House. She used to live there, before she lost.'

'Well, she near dead now – by tonight she will dead. In he meantime I calling the ambulance to carry she to hospital. Them boy knock her belly.'

'I running to tell Matron,' said Carlton. 'Matron spose to care her. She got family in America. Matron send to tell them. They coming in aeroplane – I mean in space ship.' Laughter, at Carlton's naivety rippled round. 'If she got family, where them gone?' asked one of the men. 'They left she to dead on the road. Them boy who knock this ole lady they don' know sorry. They is stranger to sorry.'

People peered down at Mama King as if she was an object from a different planet. Then they all hurried off leaving her with the market constable. It was his work to look after 'choke-and-rob' victims.

The ambulance screeched to a stop allowing the attendants access. They did their job routinely, indifferently, and yet with practised pity. 'We get plenty of these everyday. If they get money, they rob them. If they don't have money they choke them. Such is life!' they said. 'Dem boy hate old people. They spend all they young days with ole people and then turn on dem when they ole. Dey joke on dem and everyt'ing. Such, such is life.'

Mama King could hear a faraway murmuring of voices. One was her mother's. She sat on the steps of her house puffing away at her pipe and

68

talking to a knot of young women.

'I am old,' she said, 'and I am happy. Old age is a blessing. I married for forty years. My life was a life sentence to serve one man. Mabel stay good with Danny. It get better every year.' It had never got better for her. Never! Never! Never! Her mother's voice still drew her name in streaks across a vast expanse of sky. And then she was back in the home in the room again, and they all were young and happy – Tilley, beautiful Tilley, who used men as if they were spoons of sugar that she soon forgot about, and Turvey with the razor-grass tongue, and Dolly McAbe who no longer spoke. They came and smiled at her and then vanished into a dome of dense smoke. Then Danny came and leant over her and touched her face and smiled. 'Come,' he said, 'Come away with me.' He took her hand but his was so cold, she drew back from him, and he ran off before she could speak.

XV

Mama King lay in a coma in the intensive care unit. Her daughters had cabled funds and she was to be given the best of care. A group of reporters hungry for a story hovered about outside. Among them was Jake Roper who had got hold of Matron Trask as she entered the hospital and was doggedly questioning her.

'Where was the old lady these five weeks? You should have known. You failed in your duty for five weeks. Would you do that to an old white woman?' A tinge of red blood appeared under Olga Trask's rouge.

'The old woman went for a walk and lost her way. We had police looking for her. Ask Sergeant Elder.'

'But where was she?' persisted the reporter. The bangles the Matron wore to advertise her wealth, clanged and clashed like cymbals as she waved her hands and shook her fists at the persistent men.

'We have a liberal place,' she yelled. 'Not a prison. The old come. The old go. We don't lock up nobody. Why you people making trouble? Your talk is troublesome like rough-broke glass.'

'But where in hell was she – a woman of seventy-odd years old?'

'When she wake up she will tell us,' said Matron Trask. 'She got a little confuse but she will give you two cents for a shilling if you give her half a chance. She is sixty-nine years old. I won' be bullied, or cowed or beaten down by two-by-four whippersnappers. Her daughters know her so well they would cook and don't give her to eat.'

Part of Mama King was already pushing its way back into light like a shoot growing out of the earth. She tossed about in the bed looking for Cindy when she ran off, after a good, hot beating.

70

'Buy a new broom Mama, buy a broom!' came Cindy's voice.

'I don't have money Cindy. I have me last two dollar.'

Cindy suck her teeth. She snatch up the broom and start a sweep.

'I feel so shame, me mouth open. The man see his chance!'

'The broom no new no more. I can' sell it. You must pay two dollar, fifty cent and keep the broom.'

'He wouldn't go. He keep on saying the same thing over and over again like a sailor parrot. In the end I pay, beat Cindy and she run away. When I find her, we eat coconut rice and drink sage tea for three days. No money to buy flour to make bake, or oil to fry them. Then Token money come just in time.'

The reporters again pushed forward but Sergeant Elder, standing protectively beside Olga Trask, sent them home.

Mama King was now sitting huddled against Sumintra beside a high wall. The sun was quite high and when they stood up, the rags they wore threw such weird shadows that they laughed, and repeated their performance. Sumintra sang a strange song and spun round and round while the tatters of material spun out. They laughed again and again.

The bed shook suddenly with laughter and Mama sighed and blinked.

'Hm,' she muttered. 'Me head. Mule kick me head.'

A nurse rushed over and shouted to a doctor who rushed in. There was a flurry of activity and much concerned discussion. The doctor seemed relieved that she had come back to them and spoke of her resilience and will to live. The nurse quietly said, 'Lord how wonderful are thy works.'

Each day Matron had visited the hospital and the fear of recrimination seemed to have reshaped her body. She too had aged in the last few days, and even the make up and Sunday clothes could not conceal the pain in her heart. She had sat by the bed waiting for a flicker of life and was as excited as the medical staff when it came. They would not permit her to approach the bed and she sat dejectedly outside the door.

'Whatever you do for the old is never enough. They come in here, kicking although you don't see it, screaming although you don't hear it. When they accept us, they surrender their will and their spirit. Mama King didn't surrender anything. She is her own woman.'

71

Slowly she rose, leaving an untidy heap of flowers and fruit beside the chair and made her way back home, deciding to put a brave face on things. As soon as she entered her office a cable from Mama King's daughters caught her eye. An entire retinue of family were coming home.

What had she done she asked herself, to deserve this trouble. She thought of her own mother and a flaming rage swept through her, demolishing the façade of love and admiration of her mother she so often professed. She remembered how, believing her mother had hidden money, she kept her hungry and ignored her for days on end. She could see her mother's hands meddling in the life and mixing the ingredients to suit herself. She heard her mother's voice ruthlessly persuading her to give herself to a drunken world-weary degenerate when she was just sixteen years old. She could hear the warning:

'"Never go back to Africa. I humiliate myself to give you nice hair and skin. Never go back to Africa." I run away from her, from her interference – from her grasping, clinging nature. How I hated that woman! I never shared a joke, a good time or a good thought with her. Where I would be without my grandmother only God knows. I remember the day my mother come for me to sell me. I prove. Me grandmother wash it way for me. I never prove again. I hate that woman. If she didn't die, I would kill her.' She looked round to make sure she was not overheard.

Her lips quivered and her hands tightened around the pen on her table. There was a hard gleam in her eye. At that moment she strangled her mother.

'I look after these old people to find peace from what I feel in my heart. But they ungrateful too. They see me as the money-changer that Christ curse. I hate that woman and her ways! All my life I have to say I love her to please this place – to please this world.'

A kid bleated incessantly by the door for the attentions of its mother and Matron dropped her head on the table and wept at the memory of hers. She heard footsteps and hurriedly dried her tears.

Carlton came up from the laundry, tapped gently on her door and entered. 'I got to carry Miss Ginchi to hospital. I can't come to work tomorrow, Matron,' he said.

'What wrong with her?'

'She got boil here.' He pointed to his breast. 'She put poultice on it. It won't go way. It hurt she more. She got to go to doctor. Why that goat kiddy bleatin' so much? It must be hungry and want suck. I see the mother kicking it this morning. She want to wean it.'

'Well, awright Carlton, if you gran got to go, she got to go.'

'Me tell Miss Ginchi 'bout Mama King. That we find she, and that she wake up now. Miss Ginchi want to go to see she but the hospital people say no.'

'Perhaps she can talk to Mama King. Tell her to come back here to wait for her daughters. They coming you know?'

'Aunty Cyclette, Miss Ginchi say, she hot like pepper sauce,' warned Carlton.

'She-a Markey mother. Markey coming too?'

'By the sound of it, they all coming. Well, I going home. On Thursday I coming back. I miss one day money.'

'Not if you kill that kid and skin it before you go.'

'Why you killin' it – it just want to suck.'

'Kill it,' she yelled. He went out into the darkening day and soon she heard the jangling of the implements he would use.

Matron Trask took the picture of her mother from the wall. She looked hard. She looked beautiful. She looked indifferent. Matron sighed and reached to hang it up again, and missed the nail. The picture fell at her feet, the glass weirdly splintered. 'Oh God!' she said. 'Somebody going to die on me. Must be Mama King! Oh God, let it be Miss Turvey.' She felt as if death itself had walked in, and was seeking those whom he thought most ready for the journey with him.

The telephone rang. It was Bubble Elder.

'Yes, who is it? What you want? Bubble! What you wan'?'

'Oh! The news is good?'

'She wake up. Thanks! Tell the doctor, he coulda save his

time. I been there. I know she wake up.' She dropped the telephone contemptuously and flopped down in her chair as if blood, bones and all had liquefied. She fumbled in her drawer and pulled out a flattie of rum and took a long sip and soon the silence in the room was broken by the rum gurgling its way to comfort her through the uninhibited ah-h as she swallowed. More and more, drink had begun to take her into another world. It switched on strings of neon lights in her mind and illuminated her dreams.

'God bless you, rum,' she murmured. 'You look like piss and you hot like fire. I don't know what you really taste like. All I know is that you strong and full of happy heat. God bless you rum. God bless you,' she belched self-consciously. 'God bless you, rum.'

Slowly she staggered into her room, bumping into several indifferent old people. Already there were stars of unreality in her eyes. She closed the door, sat down, and floated into the world that might have been. Then she caressed herself as the man that never came should have caressed her long ago.

XVI

The next day Carlton returned to work feeling as if his heart had been mangled. Miss Ginchi had refused a mastectomy and would surely die.

'My breas' is of no use to anyone,' she said. 'Why cut it off? I must go back to me Maker, the same way I come.' Then winking at the nurse who attended her, she added:

'My breas' was always trouble for me. Everybody else got star-apples. I got sapodillas.'

She coughed and clutched at her chest which she said burnt like flaming charcoal. Her sprightliness became a crawl and the frown which pain had placed on her brow seemed to spread throughout her whole body, but she clung to her independence with a fumbling enduring fierceness.

The thought of Mama King lying sick in hospital buzzed about in her head like an irate fly. There was something she had to confess to Mabel, before she died. For years people had said she rather than Mabel should have married Danny but he was cruel, too cruel and she would have none of him. But she loved his wife – like a sister ... and then fate had intervened and sent him drunk and staggering to her door. He was accompanied by Esteban, the Amerindian from up-river, and she schemingly entertained them with white rum and souse. Esteban had brought bush rum to sell – strong, good, man-killing bush rum. She encouraged Danny to drink many bottles of it. All through the fateful night. When she tried to raise him at one o'clock he was cold and his skin lifeless and rubbery. They wrapped a canvas sail around him and carried him to Esteban's boat. It was a short and desperate journey across the shadowless sand. The branches of the mangrove trees motionless, in the windless night, stood like an army spellbound at what it had seen. She watched as Esteban sailed away rupturing the shadows thrown by those boats that still

75

waited for their owners to return. Esteban looked back and waved a paddle and she knew all would be well. They never spoke of Danny again, except to swear to Mabel that he had gone to Aruba to look for work. He deserved to die for the way he tormented his wife – a comely, peaceful woman whose innocence of life made her so eager to suffer. Miss Ginchi felt no remorse not even when she played the game of 'work and Aruba' with her friend, but it was right that she should tell all now.

Every step to the hospital was like an orchestral instrument contributing its part to a symphony of pain. Her pain was so complete, so all-pervading she thought of it as beautiful. It was her pain – tailored by fate to fit her frail body. Step after painful step led her to the place where Mama King lay.

'Ginchi,' she said. 'I know you come. I smell you smell.' Miss Ginchi took her friend's life-roughened hand in hers – frailer and weaker by far. 'Mabel, I am telling you God's truth about Danny. He dead. Bush rum kill him. He drink himself to death. Buckman would a tell you but he dead too.'

Mama King turned her face to the wall. It was as if nothing was spoken – nothing was heard. Nothing was being said that she did not already know. Then suddenly she faced Miss Ginchi. Their eyes made four.

'Me, Ginchi Thorley, kill the swine. He was a brute. All he ever do is to break women will, break women back, and drink rum.' She inched her way out of the room, down the long corridor and the narrow steps and out of the building. She stopped, and coughed as the pain shoved her towards the place where Carlton waited for her.

'Get a taxi-car,' she breathed. 'Carry me home.' The car sped along an avenue in which clean trees and poinsettias were in full bloom. 'This is the last time I seeing flowers, Carlton. You know I plant flowers, handle them, look at them, pick them but I never see them.'

In bed at last she felt peaceful. The room was quiet. Some shadowy forms entered. She knew them all. They were dressed in the best clothes they ever had. Only Danny was dirty with vomit on his shirt.

76

'Hey Danny, I had to give you twelve glass before you go,' she smiled. 'Twelve glass to kill a brute! Who is that behind you? Ben Le Cage! You dead and leave you white lady wife? And Tilley, and Joe-Joe, and Casey. All you people come back for me. And you, Buckman, me apprentice devil! What you doing on that tree. Buckman they bury you naked?'

She held both hands out but drew them back alternately saying 'No, Danny! Not you Buckman.' She held them out again and with an ecstatic smile said 'You, yes, you.' Then she gave a long gentle singing sigh, contorting her face and twitching at the same time. Then she was still.

Carlton started to shake her. For a time he was too numbed to speak. Only this morning she had been asking, 'What will you do when 'am gone?' Then she had sung,

'When I say mama, my mama come running.
When I say papa, she come as well.
My grandma was a woman
My grandpa was too. That's true!'

They had laughed together. Now he was crying alone. He drew the blinds, turned the pictures to face the wall, and put out all her plants and flowers. He was too shocked to cry. Miss Ginchi had gone to her maker.

She had forbidden a 'fancy wake and a fancy funeral.' 'I won't go to heaven,' she said. 'A few worms, plenty ants and ground beetles who care, would pick the flesh from my bones. They will eat till they little drum-bellies bust.' How the neighbours knew he couldn't tell but soon the house was full of people talking about her and lamenting her passing.

They buried her the next afternoon. She had many friends to mourn her. She had never married, never borne children. Where she got Carlton no-one knew or cared. He had been her grandson for as long as anyone could remember. He had always lived with her and accepted his life with her, and she had died, while Miss Turvey much older and weaker went on living. He opened her trunk in the gaze of the visitors. There were her Sunday clothes – her black dress with the gored skirt, her lace blouse and her feathered hat. In a pillow case were her Sunday shoes and a jam jar with a few dollars in it; and the smell of mothballs. There were some letters too.

Outside the night came closer. The window of her room remained closed. Miss Ginchi with her pittance of strength had not opened it that morning.

A few crickets chirruped, and a few frogs croaked. Only humans were aware of change and death and feelings of loss, of anger and deceit. Then a clear memory crept out of Carlton's consciousness. It was if unseen hands were drawing strands out of his mind's eye. One of the letters was clearly signed 'Your true Danny.' He recalled the visit to the hospital. He shook his head saying 'There's plenty Danny in the world.' His next task was to tell Mama King that her lifelong friend had died.

For a moment he debated with himself – would she be frightened at the news of death? Would she be afraid of ghosts? Only once had he heard her talking of ghosts. She said, 'I lef' the kitchen door open, then a cold, cold wind come – and the door shut we-e e-e -eh.' He still remembered the certainty of her eyes and the solemn way in which she mimed the closing of the door. There was no fear in her eyes – just certainty that her brother had come back, and Miss Ginchi had replied, 'Don't talk stupid – dead people get eat up by worms and ants. They never come back. Dust to dust.'

Even as she lay suspended, between being lost and the coming of her destiny, Mama saw Death and Life, both children of the same father, both legitimate. Death, dominant and conclusive. Life uncertain and accidental, friable as dry earth, malleable as clay, and finally fragile as gossamer in the hands of Death.

She was a girl again, walking fearfully past the overgrown cemetery, its wildness underlining the reluctance with which the village people went close. She watched open-mouthed at the bewildering cloud-white plumpness of the stone-carved cherubs and angels, their wings outspread, their arms reaching up at the nothingness of wind and weather.

'Why no black angels Mamma?'

'Only white go to heaven. We come to hell when we born and we go to hell when we die.'

'Look at them angel face, Mamma. So fat, so cold, so happy. The cook and nurse does come out of the grave to look after them?'

'Who know, my chile? Who know?'

'Black people only have wood-cross to mark they place, Mamma. Why Mamma? It soon fall down. Ants eat it or it rotten and fall down.'

'We all is dust, chile. Only some don't know it.'

Death came close – blacker than black. Life's eyes explored her like a reluctant lover while Death reached out for her hand, now clean with care, now slightly softened from disuse. She retracted her hand like a turtle its head. Danny sat, his face hidden in a half darkness, his body trapping the beam of light that leapt in from the window. It was as if something shone inside him.

The shaft of light streaked across the bed, its phallic form touching all that was vital in her – magically reconstituting and reawakening her – making her whole again.

XVII

For the first time in a long life, Mama King was aware that things were being done to her, or given to her, or taken from her. Nurses administered potions and pills, fed her and washed her. Doctors examined her, and investigated the working of her life-worn body. Although she watched with the curiosity of a child, worry sneaked out of the corners of her mind to torment her. Regret for the cursory care she had given her children made her restless. Work had been the culprit that wrecked her life, robbed her of her perspicacity and deprived her children of her love. Things were different when her life was given over to the care of her grandchildren. Somehow she had less energy but they had more care. Grandchildren brought time, and ease and a quiet flow of happiness. She told them stories and played with them. She did not need to conquer and control them. She laughed and they laughed when she said:

'Over the copper forest, over the iron mountain, over the stormy sea, there was a rich King monkey who had soft teeth.' Out of a radiant corner of her mind voices suddenly called out, 'Go on grandmother tell us more.'

She could see a crowd of faces behind the voices. It was as if they were under chalky water looking up at her. She sat up in bed but the faces had vanished. Miss Ginchi's grandson Carlton walked in and sat down. He took her hand and said, with little emotion, 'Grandma Ginchi dead and bury yesterday.'

She did not speak. Her eyes moved slightly.

'I miss her, I miss her talking and her rowing. I miss the food she used to cook,' Carlton continued. 'I miss her putting on her good dress on a Sunday. I have nobody in the world for family.'

'Don't cry. You got me when I get better. You can live with

me. I got a house. I still have a house? I will give you it when I dead. You take it.'

'Yes, Mama Ginchi and me clean it few weeks back. Poor Mama Ginchi, you know I never think she would ever go away. When they put her in the grave my heart get cramp. The grave was full of water. They bale out the water with a bucket from church. It had plenty tadpole and dead grass. The water colour like ginger beer.' Mama King listened. Only her eyes showed emotion, by the way she closed them or opened them as he spoke.

'She had a nice service. They sing Onward Christian Soldier.'

'Hm.'

'She had plenty wreath. Nice flower. She did like flower, yaller.'

'Hm.'

'I wish you did come. Plenty people come.'

'Hm.'

'I think I going away from here. Where she get me from? She never tell me. I wish I had mother. I would be able to go there now.'

'When the big drought come and rice burn up, she catch some people thiefing food from she farm. When they see her, they swim cross the trench, run away. They lef' you under some bush. They never come back for you. She never see they face or know they name. That's how you come. They wasn't much to tief but these two young people find something. They was good people because they run away and didn't turn roun' and cuff her down.'

Carlton raised his eyebrows at the news of his history and said, 'She was good to me. She give me everything. She was good to me. I got plenty to thank her for. She could leave me in the sun to dry out. But she take me! She save me! She was father and mother for me. I goin' way. I can' live in tha' house no more.'

'Hm.'

'I going Mama King. I never going to see you again.

81

Goodbye!'

'You can cope wid de worl'?'

He nodded. 'I think I can. I don't wan' too much. Just food and work.'

He walked out of the hospital, confident that he would see the world through his own eyes and through those of an indomitable woman. He would walk cautiously on his own feet, testing every rock and stone before putting his weight to it as she had done. He would grasp life with padded hands – hands padded with caution and experience of a life well-lived. A new kind of strength surged through him and he knew then he had grasped his manhood. 'Be a good man,' she once said. But what was a good man? He had heard talk of Danny and Ben Le Cage. He had met other men. But were they good? He did not know. Maybe a good man gives his seed to many women. Maybe he works hard as the women do. Maybe he does not work at all. Manhood is strength? He had always been a donkey-boy. Yes, manhood is strength. He had never thought of himself as a man before. Just Miss Ginchi's grandson. A donkey-boy who was happy to help and oblige.

He went back to the house and started putting his few things together. The house was quiet. There were no relatives to hang around and celebrate the death for days on end. The kitchen smelt of Miss Ginchi's last meal, the bedroom of her medicaments and the lavender water she liberally used, and the sitting-room of all those people who had laughed there, as they listened to her talk and her stories. He lit a candle and placed it by the bedroom window. Was it a symbol of the searing sadness he felt when he thought of her? Was it the star of her loyalty and kindness – a star that always burnt so brightly?

'Ow, Mama Ginchi, whey you gone? Whey you gone?' He cried until the surge of anguish receded.

Then he remembered the chickens. They had not been fed. Half-heartedly he fetched rice and corn and threw it for them. Sadness was in his voice as he called them. They came hurrying and pecked ravenously. It did not matter who fed them corn. Only the dog seemed to sense the final nature of the parting from his mistress. He howled and ran off into the night. 'Buller,' shouted Carlton. 'Buller come back!' But it sat alone upon the shadow-stricken grass, raised its head to the stars and continued its plaintive howling.

Carlton noticed lights in Mama King's house. 'Surely,' he thought, 'she was still in the hospital?' He went over to investigate.

'Who's that?' he called. 'Mama King!' The door opened almost at once.

'Hi, Carlton,' Markey shouted. 'Hi, it's good to see you. Come in! Our family are all here. Come in.'

'Hi Carlton. Remember me, Solo?'

'Hi Carlt', greeted Cindy.

The two older women continued their discussion as if nothing else existed in the whole wide world. In spite of the luggage that stood all around the little room, Carlton found a place to sit. He overlooked the changes brought by time and money. He overlooked the differences caused by living in a more demanding society. He smiled and his thoughts were of a time that for him alone had stood still.

'We're here to see grandmother,' said Markey. 'Solo, Cindy, Chuck, Mother and Auntie. Remember them?' He indicated the older women and ran on, 'Isn't it terrible the things being said about us? The papers have said some real cockamimy things about us! We got to duck out. We can't even to go to the hospital. We're lying low.' The older women looked at Carlton as if he was from the planet Mars. His barefootedness struck chords of poverty and distant times. His lack of sophistication epitomised all that they had left behind.

But Carlton was delighted. For him friends that were family had come home and in his imagination brought excitement and riches. His heart jumped about inside him, like a playful kitten every time he looked at Solo and Cindy. He barely knew the older women and Cindy's husband was a true stranger to him. But he had played games with the three youngsters and then fate and distance and time suspended their friendship.

'Solo, Boy, you can make operation 'pon people? You a real doctor?' he queried. 'You should a been here to help Miss Ginchi get better. She find me you know under bush at Bamboo Grove when I little baby.' His grief made him loquacious. He talked on about everything, asking, laughing, commenting but never once listening.

It was as if no time at all had passed. There was no meaning to change and the function of passing years. He was caught in a time warp. And his life went on. 'She find me, you know,' he said again. 'I could dead, but she take me and learn me to make me hand work for me.'

Neither Solomon or Markey could reply. They introduced Cindy's husband Chuck, a square-built, ebullient man whose body seemed to be entirely composed of contentment, good feelings and globules of dancing fat. His teeth were large, rectangular and polished, giving his smile a well-meaning commercial look. Carlton started recalling old times. The stories came like thread from a spool and the laughter like running water. They drank Cokes and ate chocolates, but Carlton pushed them aside saying, 'Me don' like them. Give me good 'guana curry any day. Remember that Markey? Remember how we use to cook guana egg? The skin, green and rough on the guana never change when it cook.'

At last he rose to go home. As he opened the door the air was suddenly charged with the smell of burning.

'Help!' a voice cried, 'Fire! Fire! Oh me Gawd Miss Ginchi house ketch fire. It burnin' down!'

'Oh God,' yelled Carlton. 'Miss Ginchi house burnin' down!' Another voice echoed the dilemma. 'Miss Ginchi house burnin' down.' Everyone dashed outside. The fire had taken hold. The flames leapt and pirouetted in an all-engulfing dance. And the sparks flew like stars without a heaven, content on turning everything they touched into an inferno, while the heat formed a wall around the house as if to defy attempts to subdue the flames. People with buckets of scarce drinking water were useless before the raging flames. The women, determined to save another woman's home, slashed at

84

the flames with the water but after many hours, where a house full of memories of life with an enigmatic old woman once stood, grey ashes formed a large sore on the earth, and burning wood sent whiffs of smoke to dance upon the breeze.

'Is me fault,' Carlton said bitterly, 'Me lef' the candle dere. It catch the blinds. The blinds catch the house.' He stood dazed and tired. 'Me put the candle! The blinds ketch fire! The wind blow the fire!' he muttered again and again. There was nothing retrievable. Nothing was left to say there was love and laughter there, and generosity and friendship and commitment. 'She find me, you know? She coulda lef' me dere to dry out. But she take me,' he said over and over again. And the wind wafted it away.

The hens, disturbed by the fire, half-heartedly roamed the perimeter of the ashes unconcerned. It was neutral territory now, and soon the grass would grow again. But something tangible had taken place inside Carlton's heart.

Neighbours came to stare at the ruins of Miss Ginchi's house. They could not understand how things had gone so wrong for either her or Mama King. They had envied Mama King her little house, her gifts from abroad, the pictures she showed of her grandchildren. Then they envied her the care that had been bought for her, but she had ungratefully run off to go with the poor, to be happy with the starving poor. 'Funny woman. Is because she old!' they said. 'She choose starvation! Stupid woman! She run away and make Miss Ginchi get sick and dead. Now poor Miss Ginchi house burn down! Is Mama King make it.'

A few kept away from the house lest they too would get tainted by stupidity. They might even catch cancer. You never could tell. They watched the comings and goings from a distance and whispered to each other, 'Mama King family come? They find she already, but she won't live one day in America. The cold will make she bleed to death! You can't pull up old tree root and plant it again.'

Then they went about their work wondering but finally accepting what life had brought to them all.

XVIII

Most of all Matron feared a confrontation with Mama King's daughters although she talked freely of throwing them out 'like pig-food.' However, she began each morning by expecting them. Her eyes were glued to the road leading to the house. She had a clear view from the window, and when she was alone, practised various forms of repartee to the mirror in her room.

Then nature took a hand. It started to rain with uncanny regularity. Each morning between ten o'clock and midday the sunlight would be overtaken by a shower, and while they struggled for supremacy old Miss Turvey would sing out, 'Rain a fall and sun a shine. Devil an' he wife a fight for ham bone.' The others would ignore her and go on with their dreaming.

It was on such a morning, after Matron's pervasive authority had touched everything, that two dripping wet women pushed the door open and walked in. They dripped little pools all over the floor, and the drops chased one another until they became a dangerous smear.

One was about six foot – tall for a woman but not fat – just well-built, staid and respectable. She seemed to have spent years reaching up for status which constantly eluded her. She walked in measured steps as if walking was a task set her, in order to assess her true worth. Matron had imagined Token soft and gentle and gullible, but here she was – without any familiar mark by which to identify her. If she was lost in a crowd of ordinary people, it would be difficult to find her except for her height.

Her sister was almost as tall, but thick and tumultuous, with a kind of seething energy that was just off boil. There was no grace about her, and her limbs appeared ready to break away from her body and take on lives of their own.

Her mouth seemed as ready to go off as a cocked pistol and her eyes swept the room from time to time, burning into Matron like a flame-thrower in a field of weeds. She made sure that her unfriendliness, mistrust and disregard were felt and seen.

Matron's dog growled. It often growled at visitors. Cyclette kept on chewing.

'What you done with my mother's self-respect?' she asked in a smouldering voice. 'You made her feel so bad about herself, she cut and run.'

'That's right,' said Token. 'Mama is difficult but you should have done better by her. We paid you. Mama was so unhappy.'

'Not always,' said Matron tentatively. 'She went outside and lost her way. The Down-and-Outs encouraged her go.' She avoided the word 'beggars.'

'No,' interrupted Cyclette. 'You made her beat it! She's going with us. You've had it! She's leaving this two-faced place.'

Matron was too confused to reply. She flopped down on a nearby chair and closed her eyes. Then she said slowly:

'You girls are too late to criticise my care. You turn away your mother. You brought her to me. I never burden you with my mother for any amount of money.'

A knife went through Cyclette's heart.

'Mama's going with me. I made a mistake but now I'm doing it right.'

'That may not be right for Mama, Cyclette. What will she do when you work? What will she do?' asked Token in a syrupy voice.

'You and your son come for a funeral. But Markey and Cindy say the same as me. We want Mama,' growled Cyclette.

Token began to pace the floor and very nearly fell where the dog had pissed. For a time no one spoke. The silence said everything. At last Token said, 'My sister is accusing me! We better hear what my Mother wants. After all, we had to accept what she said and did. She always did what was best for us.

87

And I am here to say that sometimes her "best for us" was plain dumb.'

After they had gone, Matron felt violated. She had to suffer insults from creatures like those! She had to sit there and actually listen to them! 'Lord,' she said. 'What I do to deserve "them"!' The last words slipped off her tongue as if it was phlegm.

'Comfort me, Sarah. Comfort me,' she wailed. Sarah Douglas put her arms round Matron. She was at last acknowledging that her needs were the same as the people she cared for and that her harshness with them was an attempt to build fortifications against the relentlessly encroaching tide of her own old age.

For the first time she felt suicidal. She thought of her mother as a source of wisdom and experience also for the first time. What would she have done? She would have coped by pushing everything away from her. One by one the reasons for putting an end to herself began to fall away. She saw her work as it was – exacerbating, instead of healing – a kind of grand larceny in which her accomplices were drugs and people willing to administer them. For an instant she felt shame and then that too was gone and she was left with the house of the old – Frangipani House. She too had no choice. There was nothing to do but carry on. She picked up her dog, and hugged it till it yelped.

'They will come back,' she said with rigid certainty. 'Black people does fly up and then they fly down to settle on the eggs they addle themselves!' All the feelings that hung around her like weights disappeared. She was now remorseless and could deal with anything. Frangipani House was the best eventide home in the world.

Carlton came to help in the laundry for the last time. 'I want to see everybody before I go. I taking the road. Who can tell? One day I might end up with Markey and Solo in America. Solo is doctor now. When he married Nurse Carey I can go and be yard-boy for them.'

'Yes, you a born worker,' Matron said scathingly. 'You got

the shape and the shoulder. You is a born mule. Yeah! Yeah!' she said mimicking Markey. 'Baby take it away.'

When he pretended to smoke a large cigar, Matron looked at him with horror in her face.

'You fool,' she yelled. 'Get out.'

'Why you calling me fool. I will show you one day. I'll show you.'

He broke into a punching melody, swayed in a lumbering dance and walked out.

She watched him clear the compound and then turned her attention to Carol Carey who silently watched.

'What this I hear, 'bout you getting married? You hardly know the man. He just come here?'

'I know him well. So does my family. You row your boat, and let me row mine, Matron, if you please.'

Matron continued to buzz around like an aggravated queen bee. She had drawn in from the reproach of the young nurse, the way a baby turtle draws in its head. She whispered to herself, 'God give me faith! Give me faith!' as she thought of all her troubles – Mama King, Bubble Elder, Frangipani House, Carlton, all worrisome and now Nurse Carey would have to be replaced.

'I won't let any of them paint me into a crack in a wall.'

XIX

The news spread quickly. Carol Carey was getting married to Solomon Coombs who was an eye doctor who was Mama King's grandson.

'What she getting married for?' asked Miss Turvey. 'Me and Richey live together thirty year. We had six children, I think, but we could never afford to marry one another. Whenever we scrape money together, the children want something for their belly, they back or they foot. What she getting married for? What she going to America to marry for? Wher' she want wid a t'ing like dat?'

'Oh, it good! Married good!' said Old Mother Dickson whom everyone called Titsy. 'Dickson always ask me to married him but he would really own me. He will get a certificate to say he do.'

'Only white people married! They got to married otherwise the men can never grown to be men. They stay boss all the time. And boss is never man. Ask Matron.'

'Ask Matron what?' said Matron in the peremptory manner in which she sometimes spoke to the old people.

'You ever married, Matron?' asked Titsy.

'Yes, Miss Titsy, when I was sixteen. My mother make a match for me. He was old enough to be my grandfather but we owe him money. So I married him. Every night he used to drink. He never beat me. He just drunk. Rum choke him. The day he died was the happiest day of my life. I went in the bedroom and cry from joy. Then I dance. My grandmother come in and we dance together. That's how I get money to go to America. I came back when my mother get sick, to live this life, a stagnant rotten life in a hole full of beetles crawling and complaining.'

'Beetles can't talk, Matron. Don't call us that!'

'Don't bother about black beetles. Think about the

happiest day of my life, Miss Turvey.'

Matron saw the consternation on Carol's face, and felt a quiver of feelings which she could not name.

'Don't listen to me, Nurse Carey,' she said jocularly. 'You and Solo will live like Isaac and Rebecca.'

She regained her lapsed authority, and went out into the garden to cut flowers for Mama King's room. Then she proceeded to tidy up, turning out the clothes and deciding which pieces to sell, and which would just disappear. She felt deep inside herself that the old lady would not return, but she still, still waited.

She telephoned Bubble Elder with promises of her company for as long as time allowed, as she needed him around in case Cyclette proved too physical for her. Everytime she thought of Cyclette she shook her head as if freeing it from something too terrible to comprehend. She understood Token – so full of right things, right ways and right attitudes. She seemed to be made of clay that could always be re-used, and still find some way of avoiding the kiln. Matron understood Token's shimmering primness for which two good men had valued and loved her. As Matron of the home she had independence for which men feared and shunned her. They saw no reason why they should protect her, share with her or include her in any of the games men play with women.

Bubble Elder admired her body – mostly its even golden colour. He often said, 'I respect your brains very much. It's a pity I can't sit here and watch it working for you.' She was sure that he too would like to lick her the way the dog did. That way he would worship the colour of her skin.

She had never experienced tenderness, appreciation and loving care – all that she was paid to give to the old, discarded women in her charge. Her passage to womanhood involved no ecstasy or tender words of love, or physical delicacy – just searing pain and the breath and anxious fumblings of a drunken old man.

In the past weeks she had come to understand her life and her self. She felt deeply grateful to Mama King for all the problems she had brought. She hoped with all her heart that the old lady would come back but would it not be better to visit her and tell her so? She felt sure that she could help the old lady to free herself of her daughters' belligerent concern for her welfare. She would say to her 'Be my mother. Stay here free.'

She dressed with practised skill, in her deep blue dress and her blue hat with the purple ribbon, and then laden with fruit and flowers, she made her way to the hospital. Being too early she looked around the lobby at the exhibition of ethnic paintings hanging there. When at last she entered Mama King's room she stopped in her tracks. Pandit and his people had pre-empted her and sat around the bed, quietly talking and solemnly laughing with the old lady.

'What you want?' said Mama King. 'You hard-face woman.'

'Mama King, please, all I do is come to see you.'

'I can do without you coming here.'

'Send these dirty people away. They will make you more sick.'

'You go away! You is the sickening one – you and my children plotting against me. When I go out of here, I going with Pandit. They is my family now. As soon as Doctor Case give the word, I going.'

Matron was dumbfounded. The old woman was sparky and coherent. She said what she meant to say. Her wandering mind seemed to have found a haven and although she still looked thin and frail, something about her had grown resolute and strong.

Pandit looked at Matron, bowed to her and took his leave, followed by his entourage. Mama King, alone with Matron, panicked. She remembered the thrust of the injections given her in the home and screamed that Matron had tried to inject her.

'I only put my arms around her,' Matron said weakly. 'She is like my own mother to me. I shan't come here again. I give up. She's bad!'

Mama King still sobbed and spoke incoherently about her

time in Matron's care. Then she turned her face to the wall, while Matron angrily stamped out of the room.

Mama King closed her eyes. Danny's mother had come back to ask for Token.

'Give me, me first grandchild?' she said. 'I want Token to know me! I don't want a piece-by-piece family. You ungrateful girl. I make him married you. You ungrateful girl.'

Mama King once again felt herself dragging Token back by one arm and Danny's mother pulling on the other. She heard again the people in the bus shouting 'Leh' go! Leh' go. Leh' go the woman chile.' They started stoning Danny's mother with some of the fruit they were taking to market. That's how she fell and hurt herself.

Danny was hitting her now. 'You rude to me mother! You rude to me mother.' She could feel the blows again. She started to scream 'Help!'

Ginchi came, cutlass in hand. Danny turned and ran. She never saw Danny again.

The past had become a morass in her mind, and yet it ruled her present life.

'Nurse,' she said achingly. 'Don't let Danny come in. He is a beat-crazy man. He got to beat woman. Then he is a man.'

'I won't,' replied the Nurse. 'Go to sleep Mama King. You safe with me. I give you something to make you sleep.' The drug was much more calming than any Mama King had previously been given. In answer to the need for sleep, she felt herself falling down, down, down into a strange garden full of flowers. She picked a large armful and was woken up by their weight to hear voices she did not recognise speaking in a language that she did not fully understand.

There was a crowd of people around her bed. She counted two tall men and three tall women – one taller than the rest. Some looked at her quizzically, and some with raw anxiety.

'Mama!' Token said, 'We are all here – your children and your grandchildren. This is Cindy husband, Chuck! Solo here too. He been doing great.'

'Mama, this is me, Markey. I told you I'll be back.'

'Mama, don't you remember me? Your first grandchild. Solomon. The one you used to call Solomon Grundy.'

Their voices came to her with a persistence that disconcerted her but she managed a noncommittal smile. They pushed forward, pleased that she had regained consciousness.

'Mama, you coming home to America with me,' said Cyclette. 'I am not leaving you to cut and run again. I'm not having you ill-treated by trash-beggars.'

'Cyclette, the only real kindness I ever get was from beggars. They was kind. They was good – sharing, protecting – giving me respect and friendship. They have little but they give a lot. They give me back my senses because they treat me like I was somebody. Their heart shine out to me like clean clear glass. What give you the right to criticise my friends?'

'Mama, you coming home with me,' said Cyclette again. 'I now ain't leaving you at the mercy of some tin-horn matron.'

'Cyclette,' warned Token. 'Don't raise Mama hopes. She has to go back to the home. You can't look after a cactus for a million dollars, how you going to look after Mama? Markey grow by the Grace of God. What did he do when you do two jobs to get money? Hang around us. You're as reliable as a ten-cent saxophone. And what about Charlie? You didn't even know he got shot for dealing in dirt?'

'You callin' me a rejecting mother?'

'I ain't calling you anything – just placing some facts on your plate – telling it like it is.'

'My moma was good to me. She saw me through High School,' said Markey. 'Mind you mouth! I didn't want College.'

'And you mind how you talk to my moma. She's a friend to this entire family,' said Solomon. 'Look at her. Her youth is gone. Work has scrawled its name all over her. It owns her. Do you all think about that at all. We're a family.'

'You should talk Solo. You got Uncle Abel money in your pocket.'

'Some family,' said Cindy. 'I'm on the verge of family life. There's Chuck listening and our baby listening. My baby coming into a family that look upon great-grandmother as a burden. What a family!'

94

'We've got to find our own solutions for problems like these,' said Chuck.

'We are dealing with those situations as if they are problems. We are trying Caucasian solutions. We have to go back to the African village for answers. The old in Africa have a place and a function. They are never cast aside. Ask Mama what she wants and she will tell you.'

'I know what my mother needs. Her wants don't concern me. My wants never did concern her. I could want her like hell. She had my needs to consider. Don't you talk Africa. This isn't Africa. It's a problem.'

'You're hard Token! You're hard,' said Cyclette. 'Mama is coming with me. You wish her dead, you will kill her if she gets to be too much trouble.'

'Don't talk so wild – so ignorant. I look at things beyond the here and now. In the end the home is the best place. She is there with other old people. Old and young don't mix. They like oil and water.'

Solo wore a bewildered look. He could absorb nothing besides being in love, getting married and his work with people who had unreliable vision. His dreams were so big they excluded everyone except his fiancée.

'Listen,' said Mama King. 'You all go back and leave me. I going with Pandit and Sumintra. I will stay with them I don't need much and people more than good to the old. You all get out of here with your curled up hair, you lipstick and you nice clean clothes – Git!'

'A mother can look after twelve children but twelve children can not look after a mother,' said Cindy sadly. She took Mama King's hand and placed it on her pregnant form. 'There is life in here. This life will never know you.'

'Drama! Drama!' said Token. 'Is either Africa or drama with Him and Her – the first ever Mr and Mrs.'

Quietly the baby moved and changed its shape. 'See,' said Cindy. 'It knows its own. Come with us Mama – Chuck and me.'

She shook her head.

'I free and happy with Pandit them. They never give me what you all call love, but what is love? They care for me, befriend me and bring me away from the fiercety woman. I used to sit in that place till my brains addle. I used to talk to meself – see dead people, dream funny dreams. When I run away I was happy. I go forward. I never look back. Life was risky. It like going to catch fish at high tide on rough water. I going with Pandit them.'

'You going to the home, Mama,' said Token firmly. 'I pay and I sing the tune.'

A nurse came into the room carrying a piece of folded brown paper. She gave it to Mama King. 'A beggar man left this for you Mama King.'

'Read it to me, Nurse,' she said. 'Me don't have me specs. Me sure Sumintra sell them by now.'

The Nurse read. 'Police say to leave you by yourself. The home still want you.'

Mama King felt as if she was suddenly scorched by a hot flat-iron. She didn't speak but tears welled up in her eyes and trickled down her crinkled leathery face, and shone like oil on the back of her wizened hands.

'Where Carlton gone?' she asked quietly. 'I want Carlton. He and me could live. Both of us got nobody. I ain't going back. Matron want money. Not me. You people go back where you come from.'

'Come with us,' said Chuck. 'We will protect you from every evil – walking, talking or sitting down.'

'Especially the evil ones who wants to dispose of you,' added Cindy.

'Aunty Cyclette is all mouth,' said Solo. 'She will put Mama out in the cold winds if she gets difficult and winter is cold in New York. I can't help, I'm getting married.'

'And I got a ship,' said Markey.

Token breathed. 'I am not getting rid of anyone. I don't want to get rid of anyone but needs must.'

'You are bad Token. Don't Mama mean nothing to you?' asked Cyclette. 'Don't the past? Don't her hard work and sacrifice. What would we be without her. We took her strength – all of us.'

'Matron Trask is quite kind,' said Token.

'My mother is showing me what I must do when she gets old!' Cindy spoke with such anger that her eyes shone like two black beads. 'Come with us Mama, I beg you. Whatever will the baby do without your wisdom?'

Mama King said nothing. She had grown tired of talking. She looked at them all again. It was as if she was seeing them all through a window that had accumulated years of grime and muck. Her eyes suddenly closed. She had dozed off to ease the pain and the confusion. They waited anxiously and watched.

'She's asleep,' said the Nurse. 'She knows that she has two alternatives, Frangipani or Cindy's home. Let's hope she chooses wisely.'

'I want Danny,' Mama King mumbled, 'Danny come for me.'

'Who is Danny?' asked Cindy.

'He left her years ago. He was her husband – my father,' Token said.

'I'll make all the arrangements to take her with me,' said Cindy. 'Chuck and I will stay behind till the papers are processed. We'll wait for her, even if we have to wait till the baby is born. We are choosing her. I hope you never get old Momma. If you do, don't start counting on me.'

Token shrugged. 'Make a miracle for her,' she said. 'Give it all you got. I am tired, tired, tired, you hear. I am tired of finding and providing. For too long I have been everything to this needing, wanting, demanding family. I want *me* back! Your demands, her demands, everybody's demands at some time for some thing, have me bound up like the lianas in the jungle. I'm using my cutlass and cutting, and cutting so I can find a way out to me, my life, myself.' She turned, tossed her head and walked out for a breath of air. Then she re-entered the room and stood eyeing them defiantly.

XX

For a few minutes the room was filled only with their desperate emotions and the defiant sounds of breathing with which Mama King asserted her right to the life that had always been her own. Token's voice, cracked and worn, came again: 'I am going back to where *I* am – to where the life that is mine exists. This place is the past – the painful past. Mama never wanted more than this. This is her life, not mine. I never never wanted to be like her – her altruism sickened me. Her patience – her low, low goals. Just look at her. Worn out – worked out for nothing.'

Her words linked past and present so poignantly that Cyclette began to sob hysterically. 'There is nothing here for me either,' she blubbered. 'Nothing, nothing. Just pain and hatred of poverty, hardship and useless mud and dung, pain, mosquitoes and old age.'

Markey was now crying in sympathy with his mother. 'I loved that old lady,' he said. 'She gave all the love I never got from you Momma. She was young and fine and strong. Now, she's just a heap of old age. She is so poor. It's hard associating with poverty to this degree. She wanted little, too little, I say. She was also so giving, so content, so eager to help. She was too unselfish. A good parent is a little bit selfish, I say.'

Mama King's thoughts intermingled with their voices, spun round in her head, and then passed before her eyes in a new picture show. She could see her dead cat Brownie lying in the garden while the Johnny crow ruthlessly worked at her eyes. The crow made little noises with its beak. 'Sh! Sh!' she shouted, unable to stand the sight of Brownie's eyes in the rapier beak of a crow. Token's voice pierced her heart like a dagger.

'Since Uncle Abel dead I am mother, father and husband. I have paid a high price for this family. Over here we're rich, over there we're hard working. Because of her, I have nothing to show for my whole life. I don't belong here. Not any more,' said Token.

The crow gulped down one eye and started on the other. Mama King wanted to bury Brownie, give her a decent grave. She shouted desperately, 'John crow, John crow! Let the dead cat alone!' Brownie's insides had tumbled out into the sunlight.

'You coming Cyclette?' came Token's voice again. 'No one should make me feel like this about myself.' Cyclette moved over to where Token stood overcome by deep feelings of shame. She gave a whisper of a sigh, and clutched Token's dress as she had done since childhood when she accepted defeat or felt out-argued. She looked shorter. It was as if her body had suddenly lost its strength and suppleness. Markey inched forward, glanced at each woman in turn and then scurried out of the room. Solo leant over and kissed the old lady's face, tawny and crinkled again his own. Weeping, the women shuffled out of the room and he followed, vainly trying to find words of comfort for them all. Only Chuck and Cindy remained. In an effort to contain her anguish he put his arm about her.

'We are all in this,' he said in a voice roughened with unhappiness. 'We have all been fouled up in this rat-racing world. All of us. Rat-racing has neutralised us all.'

Startled by his words Cindy replied, 'It's the first time you've included yourself in our family experience. You saw different. You talked different – pushed us back into Africa, to what only you knew. I wish I had gone with you, seen what you saw, done the same. I might have brought Mama round to the African way of things.'

The sincerity in her voice shot through to a layer of himself which he had kept deeply hidden and from which those assertions about his time in Africa emerged to dissolve criticism and doubt. For a moment his thoughts began pulling him apart, ripping open his convictions and exposing their tenuousness. What did he really know about the tribe with whom he had lived a mere twelve-month? Was he an outsider to them? A foreigner? An American with charm, gullibility, and a camera? What had he seen of the life except through sophisticated eyes from a sophisticated country? How authentic were his judgements? Ancestors ever present stalked friend or foe in the African bush. Some were even buried in the family compound, worshipped, deified. But Nature, however she manifested herself, was worshipped too. Her gentle beauty, the intricate vigour of her wrath, the crimson violence of tooth and claw, the gossamer magic of cloud or cobwebs, these too were valued. What had he really seen of Africa with its myriad forms and faces, its contrasting designs and destinies?

The two wearing early years of his married life flitted around inside his head like a fly in search of dung. His marriage had not been a rosy spin of contentment. It was in fact an enigmatic concoction, a mix of flavours. Sweet and full-bodied as mango juice. Tangy as tamarind. Sometimes as acid as the blight-stricken lime. And every now and then, as bitter as a bite. He recalled the day he vowed to leave her as his father had left his mother. The reason no longer mattered. He simply felt the urge to take the road, to release himself from the gnawing needs of a woman and blunder on and away into other less turbulent arms. And then the baby happened, bringing with it another chance to grow love, to create new dreams and weave complex fantasies of a life that none could verify.

Mama King sighed. She had buried what was left of poor Brownie. 'She gone,' she mumbled. 'The Lord my Shepherd! Brownie dead! Token! Token! Poor Brownie! Brownie gone!'

'So has Token,' Chuck said firmly. 'They have all gone! The whole caboodle. They all hit the road. Markey, Cyclette, Solo and Token!'

'She was a nice baby!' Mama King mumbled on. 'A good fat baby. Only one time she sick. Give me water, give me water to drink. I work hard! So hard! And now they cross water and gone. They don't want me no more.'

'We want you Mama,' sobbed Cindy. 'That's why we still here. They expect death to take you because death takes old age. We are not death. We want you. Just get better. That's all.'

'I almost believe you,' Mama King said. Two glistening beads of tears crawled down her cheek. 'I know where I want to go. But I can't. I will have to go with you two.'

Each day they visited her in the hospital and found her a mine of information and fun. She talked without bitterness of life with Matron Trask and compared it with her life as a roaming beggar. And when at last she was ready to return to her little house, the reporters told the world that 'Loving granddaughter and husband adopt Mama King.' She was happier than she had ever been and began to dream of life and work in a new country.

It took several weeks for the papers to be processed and during those weeks Chuck and Cindy spared no pains to build up the old lady's strength, reassure her and listen to the fears she expressed about facing up to her new life.

'What it like over there?' she asked. 'What people doing all day long?'

'Just what we're doing now. Talking, working, being family.' The words 'being family' evoked lost chords of feeling in Chuck's heart. For him 'being family' had been an on-going serfdom to his mother and his younger siblings. During the day he looked after them. In the evenings his mother shared confidences with him. He recalled the unbelievable loneliness of his childhood. He felt once again the burden of his mother's concerns and resentment thickened inside him. Where was the man when the exhausted youngster needed him? He lied to his teacher about his father's work and whereabouts. He felt again the tentacles of his neglect. At this point he wanted to speak out about the joys of polygamy, about the support women give to women, and brother to brother, in that village in Africa but he held back, and smiled.

'My father had no family,' he said. 'Just sons and daughters. Now, they have children but he has no grandchildren. He just goes from place to place like some goddam hobo shouting, "I've dropped by" and "I'm taking off later today".'

'Poor man,' said Mama King. 'You young people owe him life. You should look after him.'

'Life's not about shoulds. He never looked after us. Never shared a joke, a game or a song with us. Where would we be without Momma? She could never lay out her money like the white folks she worked for. It was her one regret. Her hands had visible holes through which money fell and was lost to her forever. We never had enough money to live until we went to work.'

'Your Mama was wise, Chuck, and kind,' Cindy remarked soothingly. 'She was a good Momma.'

'And smart. One day she had no money – she took the four of us for eats at Dobinson. When we full, she suddenly found a bug in the hamburger. Mr Dobinson apologised and let us leave with the bill unpaid. I was the one she primed to holler, "a bug in the hamburger, Mr Dobinson!".'

'If you Mama was so poor, who send you to school?' asked Mama King.

'Mama King, it's called motivation!' laughed Chuck. 'You got a big engine inside you on overdrive and it keeps you going till you get there. I was lucky. I got breaks. I got encouragement too – from Cindy.'

Mama gave Cindy an approving smile. She felt certain then that she wanted to be with them.

'But when we going to get the papers? When they coming? I getting tired of the waiting. Time is passing for me,' she said self-consciously.

'And me,' replied Cindy who was close to her date. She feared having her baby in primitive conditions – without a doctor and with more than basic facilities. She too wanted home. Mama King sensed fear in her voice and reassured her.

'You born here. You' Mother born here. Everything good here. I wish Ginchi didn't dead though, and Tilley. Them two was better than any midwife, Tilley had all six with just me and Ginchi in the room.'

Chuck too reassured Cindy, but she urged him to telephone

the embassy and explain, yet again, the urgency of the visa. He listened, promised and then decided to let things take their course.

XXI

Mama King's reprieve now allowed her time for easy free-ranging reflection. Each afternoon she sat pondering the number of times that life had reconstituted her – first as child, then as woman, wife, mother, grandmother, mad-head old woman, beggar and finally old woman at peace at last.

On some evenings a parade of her contemporaries, all now dead and gone, passed before her mind's eye. She nodded with approval and frowned with disapproval at the quirks of fate and time. One gap in the record of knowing particularly troubled her. And once again she asked herself: 'Wha' happen to Julia McAbe' daughter, Tina? Tina the determined. Tina, who could conquer Duppee. Tina with the concrete heart?' She remembered the encounter with Tina when her dead brother's wife turned up like a sea-beach coconut and demanded her children. They had not heard from the mother in thirteen years – not a line, a birthday card or the wax from her ear. But one day, breezy bright and brassy she waltzed in, wrapped up in a booming squall of a man and said:

'I come for me children! I run away and lef' dem but now I come back!'

Julia McAbe was stunned. The children were her life. Tina worked and she slaved for them. The girl was congenitally a striver and a coper, the boy learning helplessness and encouraged to leave things to the women in his life. Both children were happy to leave. They suddenly found their old life intolerable. They wanted change!

'You all old enough to know, there can be no coming back here!' said Tina calmly. 'Once you walk out a that door, you never walk in again. For years I work for your back and belly. My Mama slave to keep you clean. Once you walk out, you ain' comin' back! Understand?' The children nodded and went with their mother. Two weeks later, neglected, unwashed and hungry they returned to their grandmother. But Tina chased them off even though her mother, Mama King and many other women pleaded with her. 'Hallelujah,' she said, 'I free. They ain't my children and God set me free!' Two weeks later she disappeared. 'Life is a life sentence,' she wrote. 'I prepare to serve two, one for you and one for me. With them I have to serve four. I won't live that long.'

Julia McAbe never said another word. She went quiet-crazy and ended up in Frangipani House.:

'I wonder wha' happen to Tina McAbe.' Mama wondered so hard, she did not see Sumintra coming. Sumintra was always quiet in an incomprehensible way. She came and went like an apparition, or a wind-dolly.*

'Pandit sen howdye. Everybody sen howdye. Nice how you take a long res' nowadays. You have not worry in your mind. Nowaday you mind like poor-man-pocket. Nothing inside.'

'Hm,' said Mama King. 'Poor man pocket mostly got hole.'

'Cindy get baby yet?'

'Call she and axe she Sumintra.'

Just then Cindy came out with a glass of milk for Mama King.

'Hello, Sumintra. How you doin'?'

'Good, some day! Bad some day!'

'You belly drop arready but it will drop more low when pain come. It big you know Cindy. It goin' hid you face jus' now. Maybe you get two or three pickney!'

Their voices brought Chuck to the door.

'How about triplets, honey. Suppose we get triplets?'

'That would be like having three steaks from one hunk.'

'My mother was a twin,' said Mama. 'Twin skip generation.'

The women from the lane often stopped for 'woman-talk and time-waste,' which meant discussing their own childbirth experiences.

'The pain, it hot! You never get it when you stump you toe.

*A sprite blown into shape from bits of cloud by the wind.

105

When the baby want come out, you want push. Then woosh it come out.'

'You don' remember next day.'

'When you pain start the baby get low.'

'Does the midwife give you pain-killers?' asked Cindy.

'Pain-killers! Who can kill pain! Every baby got its own pain!'

'You got to push saafly, Cindy. Push like this.' Sumintra demonstrated to the obvious delight of the others.

Cindy looked full and ready. One by one they touched her, and spoke to the baby inside her.

'Get brains in you' head not cow-guts.'

'Come easy to your mother, you hear,' one said stroking her. 'Don't cause worries.'

'Be healthy and strong,' said another.

'Good milk will flow for you.'

'Sing to the baby Cindy. Rub you belly when you sing. Call the baby. Talk to it,' said Mama King. 'It will move when you talk.'

Cindy felt strengthened and supported. 'I am so happy,' she said, 'that you are all sharing this pleasure with me. Chuck sure will get the same support from your men. Sure thing.'

'Support! They wouldn' give him support. They will give him rum – white rum, bush rum and five year rum. Shoor ting.'

XXII

Nature suddenly chose her time. Early the following Monday morning the water broke and Cindy felt the first dull murmurings of labour. The midwife a brusquely efficient woman, known among the yard-people as 'Missy New Fangle,' was brought to the little house. She set about the preparations with the same icy competence with which she pedalled her bicycle from call to call. Mama King watched hopefully but the midwife's eyes were the weapons she effectively used to discourage anyone who came close enough to sniff her profession or touch her status.

Cindy paced the room in an attempt to withstand the ever-rising tide of pain, while Mama tut-tutted at the midwife's antics, and fussed because Cindy was being 'told wrong,' in a battle-hardened and off-hand way. From time to time, the midwife emerged from the room wearing an apron that looked like a yard of cloud gathered into shape; she spoke to Chuck who relayed the requests to Mama King. At last in the manner of someone who knew the routine, the old woman opened the door and went in. 'No more waiting for the invite. Ah come to the Bacoo Barn Dance that going on in my house,' she said calmly.

'I won' be responsible for your actions,' remarked the nurse. 'This is my case.'

'And my granddaughter. You know Mama love you Cindy. You know Mama never tell you wrong. Work with the pain. Bear down like this.' She showed Cindy how.

Cindy nodded and started doing as her grandmother said.

Chuck, rigid with anxiety, stood alone in the yard. There were no men about at that time a day. Only the preacher could be heard laughing with his flock a few houses away. More then ever Chuck wished for the clinical expertise and disposable comforts of his native land. What if the conditions Cindy had

107

chosen failed her? His mother's voice stirred his memory and he recalled her fresh and undistorted by time and death.

'Keep calm!' he could hear her saying. 'Everything to God's own time.'

There was a great deal of scurrying and urgent whispering. The nurse dashed out and collected articles that had become doubly necessary.

'Mercy!' she gushed. 'It's two of them. One hiding behind the other. It's two of them. No wonder she was that size. Chuck, it's two of them!'

'One more push, Cindy,' Mama King encouraged. 'You know grandmother never tell you do wrong.' Cindy responded. The second baby came in a rush.

'What are they,' she asked weakly. 'What are they?'

'Boys,' said the midwife. 'Two boys.'

'Two generation pass,' said Mama King, 'My mother was twin. I never think Cindy would be the one. Today twin born in my house! Let me bury the afterbirth – hallelujah!'

Chuck looked about him in an effort to locate something that would give substance to his present reality. There was nothing that he could choose – only the little orange tree with its delicate branches of sweet-scented flowers. He felt the need for support at that important moment of his life. There was nothing. Briefly he recalled his father, recalled the pleasantly curled lips and those soft poetic eyes that hardened under life's abrasive hand. There was a surge of pity for Cindy, and for the pain he could not share. Yet the quality of the pity, its content and intensity were familiar. He had come to know them well through the suffering he had seen in his comparatively short life.

'I wish Momma was here and Aunty Cyclette and Solo and Markey,' Cindy sobbed. 'There is nobody else to tell.'

'Your mother is not here because she chose not to be,' Chuck said consolingly. 'I'm here with you and my sons! With my family.'

'Pride is like cement,' said Mama King. 'It fasten you to your own. Token got the wrong pride.'

'They're small,' said Chuck. 'Didn't think children could be that small. Just look at them!'

The nurse smiled. 'How do you feel being a father twice in one day. The doctor knew that there were two of them?'

Cindy nodded. 'They said that there could be, but I didn't think it could be.'

The bigger baby began fishing with its little mouth for something to suck. The other made the gentle sounds of the new-born. Chuck smiled. A new kind of consciousness began to grow inside him and forced him to shout, 'I am the father of two fine sons!'

'Yes,' said Mama King, 'You're a family now. You have everything.'

'What you saying Mama?' Chuck anxiously asked.

'Just that you don' need me. I stayin' here in this house my brother Abel buy for me.'

'Mama!' said Cindy. 'Don't play jokes on us. We need you now. Who will help me?'

'I will do the best I can,' she said. 'But,' she added fiercely, 'my heart brittle – like eggshell. It easy to break. Now what name you giving these two boy?'

'Amos,' said Cindy.

'Abel,' said Chuck.

'Show me which is which,' demanded the midwife. 'I must label them.'

Mama King smiled and nodded. 'Yes, label them. Two nice parcel that come from God.'

Glossary

1	*Backoo – Backru*	spirit, sprite
2	*Boulanger*	egg-plant
3	*Channa*	boiled Spanish peas
4	*Cockamimy*	American slang, silly useless
5	*Courida*	Guyana hard wood
6	*Crapaud*	toad
7	*Duppy (Duppee)*	evil spirit
8	*Fara-Fara*	corruption of Far Ah! or Ah Far
9	*Marabunta*	wasp, also known as Jack Spaniard
10	*Mauby*	bitter sweet home-made drink
11	*Mucka-mucka*	plant, milky juice of which causes itching
12	*Nara*	complaint caused by twisting or rupturing of intestines
13	*Rucktion*	aggressive, disagreeable
14	*Souse*	pickled pork dish
15	*Susu*	to whisper

THE AFRICAN AND CARIBBEAN WRITERS SERIES

The book you have been reading is part of Heinemann's long established series of African and Caribbean fiction. Details of some of the other titles available are given below, but for further information write to:
Heinemann Educational Books Ltd, Halley Court, Jordan Hill, Oxford OX2 8EJ.

CHINUA ACHEBE
Arrow of God
A brilliantly told story of the pressures of life in the early days of white settlement. First winner of the New Statesman Jock Campbell Award.

HAROLD BASCOM
Apata
A young talented Guyanese finds the colour of his skin an insuperable barrier and is forced into a humiliating life of crime.

T. OBINKARAM ECHEWA
The Crippled Dancer
A novel of feud and intrigue set in Nigeria, by the winner of the English Speaking Union Literature Prize.

NGŨGĨ WA THIONG'O
A Grain of Wheat

'With Mr Ngũgĩ, history is living tissue. He writes with poise from deep reserves, and the book adds cubits to his already considerable stature.'

The Guardian

GARTH ST OMER
The Lights on the Hill

'One of the most genuinely daring works of fiction to come my way for a very long time.'

The Listener

CHINUA ACHEBE
Things Fall Apart

Already a classic of modern writing, *Things Fall Apart* has sold well over 2,000,000 copies. 'A simple but excellent novel . . . He handles the macabre with telling restraint and the pathetic without any sense of false embarrassment.'

The Observer

ELECHI AMADI
Estrangement

A portrait of the aftermath of the Biafran War by one of Nigeria's leading novelists and author of *The Great Ponds*.

ZEE EDGELL
Beka Lamb

A delightful portrait of Belize, a tiny country in Central America dominated by the Catholic Church, poverty, and a matriarchal society. Winner of the Fawcett Society Book Prize.

BESSIE HEAD
A Question of Power

'She brilliantly develops ascending degrees of personal isolation, and is very moving when she describes abating pain. Her novels – and this is the third – have a way of soaring up from rock bottom to the stars, and are very shaking.'

The Sunday Times

ALEX LA GUMA
A Walk in the Night

Seven stories of decay, violence and poverty from the streets of Cape Town, and by one of South Africa's most impressive writers.

NELSON MANDELA
No Easy Walk to Freedom

A collection of the articles, speeches, letters and trials of the most important figure in the South African liberation struggle.

EARL LOVELACE
The Wine of Astonishment

'His writing is lyrical, reflecting Trinidadian speech habits as well as they have ever been reflected. This is an energetic, very unusual, above all, enlightening novel; the author's best yet.'

Financial Times

JOHN NAGENDA
The Seasons of Thomas Tebo

A pacy, vivid allegory of modern Uganda where an idyllic past stands in stark contrast to the tragic present.

SEMBENE OUSMANE
God's Bits of Wood

The story of a strike on the Niger–Dakar railway, by the man who wrote and filmed *Xala*, 'Falling in the middle of Ousmane's literary canon, before he turned to film making, it is in some ways his most outstanding, and certainly his most ambitious work of fiction.'

West Africa

NGŨGĨ WA THIONG'O
Petals of Blood

A compelling, passionate novel about the tragedy of corrupting power, set in post-independence Kenya.